Interior Design

S T O R I E S

Philip Graham

Scribner

SCRIBNER
1230 Avenue of the Americas
New York, NY 10020

Scribner and design are trademarks of
Simon & Schuster Inc.

Set in Fournier Monotype
Designed by Brooke Zimmer
Manufactured in the United States of America

1 3 5 7 9 10 8 6 4 2

Library of Congress Cataloging-in-Publication Data
Graham, Philip, date.
Interior design : stories / Philip Graham.
p. cm.
I. Title.
PS3557.R217I58   1996   96-19894
813'.54—dc20   CIP

ISBN 0-684-80372-0

The following stories have appeared, some in slightly different
form, in these magazines: "Beauty Marks" in *Apalachee
Quarterly*; "Geology" in *Arrival*; "The Pose" in *The Chariton
Review*; "Another Planet" in *Fiction*; "The Reverse" in *The
Florida Review*; "Interior Design" in *Mid-American Review*;
"Angel" in *The Missouri Review*; "Lucky" in *The North American
Review*.

The brief passage quoted in "Lucky" is from *Gray's Anatomy*.

To Grace Paley and Frederic Tuten,
and to the memory of Donald Barthelme:
splendid teachers, gracious friends

CONTENTS

I would like to express my gratitude to the National Endowment for the Arts; the Corporation of Yaddo; the Illinois Arts Council; and the Department of English, School of Humanities and Center for Advanced Study at the University of Illinois at Urbana-Champaign for generous support during the writing of this book. My deepest thanks and appreciation go to my editor, Maria Guarnaschelli, and Geri Thoma, my agent, for their many years of faith and encouragement.

You do not need to leave your room. Remain sitting at your table and listen. Do not even listen, simply wait. Do not even wait, be quite still and solitary. The world will freely offer itself to you to be unmasked, it has no choice, it will roll in ecstasy at your feet.

—FRANZ KAFKA

But then that reality suddenly turned out to be no less complex and secret, indecipherable and dark than that world of dreams.

—NATALIA GINZBURG

The real is as imagined as the imaginary.

—CLIFFORD GEERTZ

Another Planet

Because for the longest time I hated the thought of hitting any sort of ball, I always swung wildly at even the easiest pitches. So I often trudged home through the park after school, still filled with the groans and taunts of my gym class teammates. Once, trying to drown out the laughing contempt of those voices inside me, I kicked at the gravel in the path, and after all these years I can still remember how those tiny pebbles looped in the air. My little sister Molly, following me home again, watched briefly and then she stopped to examine a twig. I stood there and tramped down on the ground until I began to enjoy those curious crunching sounds. They reminded me of the clicking odometer on my dad's latest project in the basement, his machine designed to determine just how many miles a shoe will last.

I kicked again and walked on. Molly was scribbling invisible marks in her notebook with that twig and didn't notice I was leaving her behind. So I stepped faster, and then I ran a weaving route through the park, imagining that I clicked away miles. I sped past old people and mothers with their babies as if they were trees planted in the gravel path, trees with no fruit, no blossoms, no birds' nests, nothing to make me pause, and I ran until I had to kneel in the grass, my lungs heaving. I felt as if my body could not contain me, my arms and legs potential explosions, my fingers and toes flames, and as I crouched there, trying so hard to keep still, I gave in to the forbidden thought of sneaking downstairs to Dad's workshop.

When I arrived home Molly was already settled in front of the television in the living room, and while cartoons raged she clutched the ragged whisk broom she habitually preferred to her dolls. Mom was sitting at the kitchen table, preoccupied with one of her How-To books, her long legs crossed, a hand sweeping through her wavy hair.

"Where have you been, hon?" she asked, her book down, her arms out for a hug.

"Just the park," I said into her firm embrace.

"Have a good time?"

"Uh-huh," I said and slowly slipped from her arms. When she turned back to her book I darted around the door to the basement.

I waited. She hadn't heard me. So I walked quietly down the steps, guiding myself by the sun filtering through the narrow basement windows. Already I could hear a muffled clatter. I opened the workshop door, quickly closed it behind me, and I flicked on the light.

There it was, Dad's Electric Shoe Scraper. The demonstration shoe in the metal harness slowly rose and lowered onto a rotating band of sandpaper—80 grit, which Dad said was the roughness closest to concrete. The odometer ticked along, the sole and heel wearing away while the shoe went nowhere, and on the floor was an eerie halo of sandpaper shavings and leather dust.

The sandpaper was worn, and I supposed Dad would have to change it when he came home that night. I knew that when the bottom of a shoe was finally a ragged mess he clocked the total. Then

he could quote the shoe's impressive mileage to prospective customers. I closed my eyes and listened to the regularity of the
machine's clank and scrape, which Mom always said drove her nuts
when she loaded the clothes washer in the basement. I loved that
sound, but I instantly regretted the thought because I could just
make out Mom anxiously calling me upstairs as if she had read my
mind.

"Sammy?"

I heard her start down the steps. I turned off the workroom
light and waited for my eyes to adjust to the dark.

"Sammy?"

She was downstairs now, her footsteps approaching, and I hid
behind stacks of empty shoe boxes. Hunched low in the cramped
space, my hands on the floor for balance, I felt a fine grit, and I
realized that I'd left behind me a line of indicting footsteps from
the circle of dust around Dad's machine. Then I heard the door
open and the light was on.

"Come on out, honey," Mom said gently. I rose from behind
the boxes to face her disappointed eyes. I waited, but from the
way her lips were pressed together I saw that she wasn't going to
say anything further, at least to me. I was grateful for that, and
when we walked up the stairs I hoped for even the smallest glancing touch, on my shoulder or hair.

I joined Molly on the living room carpet and watched cartoons
into the late afternoon. In the darkening room the black-and-
white images cast swift shadows on our faces as a flying cartoon
fox, eyes screaming in its sockets and tail flaming, plunged to its
awful, temporary fate. Beside me Molly ran her hand across the
edge of the bristles of the whisk broom, making a dry, rhythmic
sound like a movie projector.

Mom was in the kitchen, cooking spaghetti yet again, and I
could tell from the sharp little bangs of the pots and the staccato
crunks of the can opener that she was trying to contain her anger

while she waited for Dad. My parents usually argued about why the car couldn't go into the shop this month, why we still didn't have a color TV, or how terrible it was that Molly and I had to share the same bedroom. Just the day before they had fought over the tangled web Molly made from Mom's spools of thread. Now I was sure they would soon argue over me, and I was filled with a shivery anticipation.

Dad's car slowly entered the driveway. Molly and I hurried to the window and watched, silent and motionless as if we were one child, the cartoon mayhem behind us. Dad stepped out of the car, his lips pursed from whistling some song that always stopped when he opened the front door.

"Hey, kids," he said, glancing at the TV and then bending to kiss us, "plenty of excitement tonight, huh?" We offered our small faces to his lips. As he held us his palms gave off the faint scent of shoe polish. But what I remember most about his hands were those drastically bitten-down nails, which I worried might never heal.

We heard a crash behind us and we turned to the television. The fox lay flattened beneath a boulder, its bushy tail poking out and slightly waving, like a flag of truce. Molly flicked the bristles of her whisk broom.

Dad stroked Molly's hair and she pressed her head against his hand. He punched me gently on the arm. "What's your secret today, skipper?"

That night, instead of my usual, disappointing silence I had an answer for him. "I'm sorry I went down to your workshop."

"That's okay. Didn't hurt yourself, did you?"

"No . . ."

Mom clattered a colander in the kitchen. "Well, I'll see you guys later," Dad said, and he started down the hall.

"Daddy, your shoes," Molly said.

"Oh, of course, honey." He leaned down and carefully unlaced them. They were a shiny black, with tiny air holes that Molly loved. He stepped out of one and Molly rubbed her cheek against its pocked surface. Dad called out, "Allll aboard!" and he walked off in his socks to the kitchen. Molly followed and pushed the shoes across the rug, chanting, "Chugga-chugga, chugga-chugga," racing the right against the left.

Without turning from the burners, Mom arched her head for Dad's kiss, a stiff formality that I suspected was meant only for us. Molly circled the shoes around our parents and I dawdled at the door. We both knew they wouldn't start in until we were back among our cartoons. With a significant glance our way, Mom then stared down the hallway, where she wanted us to go. Dad, as usual, was busy with some mail lying on the kitchen table.

"C'mon, Molly," I said, and she abandoned Dad's shoes in the middle of the floor with a regretful sigh.

On the television a family of mice ran from a peg-legged pirate cat, and I could just hear Mom say, "I thought you promised to lock the door to that room down there." The eye-patched cat snarled and slashed at the mice with a cutlass as they sped up the ship's rigging, and I couldn't make out Dad's reply.

"Take it to the store where it belongs," Mom said, her voice rising.

"What, and alert the competition?" Dad replied.

Mom laughed her bitter laugh. "Who else would want a machine that ruins shoes?" The mice easily jumped on the swinging blade and slid down the cat's tattooed arm. Surprised, it gaped at the mice, who huddled and prepared their next move.

"Maggie, you just don't understand, that shoe will help me sell many more."

I was nowhere to be found in their angry words and I turned up the sound on the TV. "Louder," Molly said. The mice pulled the cat's tricornered hat down over his eyes. Our faces were flickering masks, continually changing as we watched that endless cartoon feuding, where no matter what terrible things happened everyone miraculously survived.

*   *   *

As always, when dinner was ready we all sat at the table as if nothing had happened. I couldn't stand the sight of the spaghetti, which we'd already eaten twice that week, and I closed my eyes.

"These new shoe styles, who makes them, anyway?" I heard Dad complain. "Each one sells worse than the last."

"Somebody must be selling them, somewhere," Mom said, as if talking to herself.

I listened to the sucking sound of spaghetti lifting from the bowl, and when I opened my eyes I saw Mom scooping a large portion onto my plate. "Why do we have to eat this stuff all the time?" I blurted out, immediately knowing the answer.

No one replied. Molly stared at me, surprised. *She* was usually the one who made the awkward mistakes. Then Mom said quietly, "Ask your father."

But I didn't, and she repeated, "Ask him."

I stared at the spaghetti on my plate; I wanted it to disappear.

Mom couldn't help herself. "Go on, Sammy," she said, "ask him why."

"Because it's delicious!" Dad screamed at her. They were up and shouting, and when Mom cried out, "You sell things people *walk on*, why shouldn't everyone walk over *you* too?" Dad held his ears and moaned, "No more!" He ran from the room and she followed.

Molly pushed away from the table, her fork and knife clattering on the floor, but I stayed and twisted the spaghetti strands around my fork, making little splatters of tomato sauce on my plate, and I forced myself to eat as a punishment for my foolishness. This was the first time my parents' disputes had spilled into dinner, and I was shocked at what I had wrought. Even now, when I think about that night, those harsh words seem solid, as if they have always existed.

The bathroom door suddenly banged open. "Sammy?" Molly peered into the kitchen. Her arms and legs were covered with Band-Aids of all sizes, and little pink circles dotted her face. She flashed a conspiratorial grin that transformed into a mock grimace of pain, and then she ran down the hallway. I rushed after her into the living room, where Dad was roaring while Mom held out her wrists and screamed, "Handcuffs!"

Molly pushed between them. "I hurt," she cried, "I hurt!"

They stopped, amazed to see us. Mom collapsed on the couch, her hands grasping at her face, and Dad crouched down to comfort Molly. "*Where* does it hurt?" he asked.

"Everywhere!" she wailed into his shoulder.

"Well," he said, picking her up, the grim line of his mouth easing, "the Tickle Bug can fix you." Molly squealed and struggled in his arms.

Dad retreated to his workshop for the rest of the evening, Mom scrubbed everything imaginable in the kitchen, and Molly and I were left to ourselves. Later that night, after Mom tucked us in and turned off the light she lingered in our room. Suddenly she was repeating, "I'm so sorry, my darlings, I'm so sorry."

"It's okay, Mom," I murmured. Molly said nothing.

"It's just that, how are we going to manage?" Mom said. "I mean, what can we do?" She stood so still in the middle of our dark room. Molly turned away under her blankets.

"I only want the best for you both," Mom kept saying, "only the best."

"I know, Mom, I know," I replied, hoping to draw her to my bedside for one more hug. I waited. Then she opened the door and before I could say good night she was gone.

Molly fell asleep easily with a faint, satisfied grunt. Though I was still angry at her stubborn silence, I relished those pauses between her steady breathing, for it was only at such moments that I could pretend I had my own room. Finally I reached under the bed for my box of tennis balls.

Under the covers I held a flashlight between my chin and shoulder, and with a pen I drew on one of the balls. My pen sometimes catching on the fuzzy surface, I mapped out continents, river systems, and mountain chains, creating a strange world I could hold in my hand. It looked like none of the planets on the mechanical model of the solar system that spun so wonderfully when my science teacher cranked it up, and on my planet there was only one town, only one house. Inside lived my family, and spaghetti was our favorite treat. We ate and joked noisily at the table, and we all asked for seconds. I allowed no bitter words to escape from anyone. After our meal was done and we cleared the table and washed the dishes together, I put the tennis ball away under the bed with all the other happy versions of my family. I was careful to rest it only on an ocean, for I didn't want to crush anyone. How optimistic I was, to think our troubles could be solved, and yet how pessimistic, to think they could only be solved on another planet.

The next day after school I easily slipped away from Molly when she began jumping on cracks in the sidewalk, and I headed for town instead of home. I was worried about Dad and his store. It had been so long since Mom had taken us there, ever since Dad had motorized his display tables to turn in circles. "To better serve my customers," he said, but Mom claimed they just made her dizzy, especially when Molly raced around them.

I ran almost all the way, so that Mom wouldn't ask where I'd been for so long when I finally returned home. Each swift step made me feel both weaker and lighter, and to encourage myself I pretended I was closing in on somebody, though a few of the adults on the sidewalk seemed to think *I* was being chased. "Hey you, stop," someone yelled out behind me, but I never looked back, leaving behind imagined miles as my shoes slapped on the pavement.

When I arrived, heady from all that intoxicating running, I noticed something new: a little speaker above the glass door blaring out some sort of tap dancing music. It almost seemed to accompany the steady rasp of my breath. Standing there before the storefront, for a moment I felt like Dad. I remembered one rare morning when Mom dropped him off and I watched from the car as his head turned slowly to take in all those varieties of shoes on artfully arranged pedestals in the window, and above them the neon sign—Frank's Fancy Footwork. Dad loved that shoe store; I can't recall him talking about anything else. Now I think I understand why, and I can say this because I've thought a lot about it: all that brick, the wide glass panes, and the sign with his name reflected something inside him. So when he entered the store each morning somehow he also stepped inside himself, into everything he wanted to be.

My face still flushed from running, I opened the door. One of the fluorescent bulbs was out. Another flickered erratically, and the display tables revolved for the dimly lit and empty store. Dad came out from the back room, his shirt sleeves up. He stood by the cash register. He brushed back his hair.

"What's up, Sammy?"

"Nothing . . ."

"Well, you look bushed. C'mere." He whirled the rack of shoe polish on his desk counter and reached for a drawer. "Have a lollipop." Dad's were special, in the shapes of animals. He handed me a bright green octopus.

"Thanks Dad, great," I said, even though a few of the arms were broken and stuck to the clear plastic wrapper.

He took me to the back room, where orderly shelves filled with shoe boxes rose up to the ceiling. "Well, kiddo," he said, straightening a few boxes, "I'm glad to see you, I'm here all by myself today. I had to fire another salesman. A real winner, that one was. No wonder sales are a little slow. Nobody cares enough about shoes, for them it's just a job." He paused and stared at me steadily, as if I didn't believe him. I nodded.

"Y'know, Sammy"—he grinned—"I'll tell you a little secret: no shoe ever completely fits. That's why it's so important to relax your customers." I nodded again and he gestured out—toward the stool he would sit on while serving customers, and the cool metal plate that measured foot sizes.

"If a woman wants her shoes to be a size seven," he continued, "just sell her whatever fits and tell her it's a size seven. Y'see, you have to know how to fit with your customers, like they're shoes too. Praise a mother's child. If a man's been to college, draw him out about what he studied, compliment the college life. You have to share something, and quickly. A customer can say 'No' easily to a stranger, but not so easily to a new pal." He tapped his fingers against one of the shelved boxes. "It's as easy as *that*," he said.

The front door opened. A fat man looked in, wiping his forehead with a handkerchief. "Hello?" he called out, and he took a few hesitant steps inside.

Dad turned and whispered to me, "Here's your chance to see how it's done. You won't find *me* trying to sell any shoe polish before I've sold the shoes!" He set off for the showroom.

Dad stood close to the fat man, who kept backing away from one display to another. I peeked out at them, and finally the customer stopped to examine a pair of heavy, official-looking shoes, near enough for me to hear Dad say, "Those will last you over twelve hundred miles, and much longer if you do most of your walking on carpets."

"Really," the man replied. His mouth almost wrinkled into a smile, and then he moved on.

I imagined I was a salesman and, thinking of Dad's secret, I plotted my approach: I would casually mention my favorite candy bar to the fat man and discover it was his favorite too! I saw myself seated before him, tying the laces of his new shoes, while he wriggled his toes inside and we gabbed about caramel and chocolate.

"Excuse me?" I heard Dad say.

"Maybe next time." The man sidestepped Dad and bumped into one of the display tables, which stopped turning. Then, with a low squeal it lurched back into its circular motion and the fat man was out the door.

Dad flopped down into a chair and covered his face. I stood in the back room doorway, unsure what to do.

"Look, Sammy," he said quietly into his hands, "let's not tell your mother about this, okay? It's our secret."

"Dad," I said quickly, "let me help. I can sell some shoes."

"Sure, son," he said. He smiled across the room at me, a weak smile that also meant No. I turned away, determined not to cry, and I noticed for the first time an odd and irritating hum coming from the revolving tables.

I'm sure that no more than a few weeks passed before that afternoon when Molly and I came home from school and Dad was already there, sitting on the couch. His hands were cupped on his lap as if they had just covered his face, and I immediately remembered my visit to his store. Mom sat beside him and they both looked weary. When Molly asked, "Daddy, why are you home, are you sick?" they stared at us as if we were strangers.

That evening Dad didn't talk about his store and Mom didn't complain about it. But their silence had no feeling of peace, and I worried that the words they held in were too terrible to be spoken. From then on Dad was always home when we returned from school, and during dinner I almost wished my parents' arguments would start again, their quiet disturbed me so.

Waiting on line one day in the school cafeteria, I stood quietly when one of the older boys began to push in front of me, somehow certain that he was about to turn around and say, loudly, "Hey, are you some kinda poor boy now your old man's store's closed down?" I imagined that even if he laughed and shoved me I wouldn't reply, but instead he just swaggered ahead and cut in line even closer to the chicken chow mein. I considered walking into town but I didn't have to—it was terribly easy to imagine Dad's store with the window displays gutted, the neon sign shut off, and the tables inside immobile.

Over dinner that night our parents' silence continued in every tense passed plate, and the effort of their restraint seemed to exhaust Dad. His eyes wandered, and finally he said, "The most amazing thing happened at the store today."

We turned to him, our forks and knives motionless. He *was* still working, I thought. Mom dabbed at her lips with a napkin.

"Mrs. Mitchell came in today," he continued. "I saw her shoes hadn't come from my store, and, I don't know, I couldn't help myself, I said, 'Mrs. Mitchell, long time no see.' She didn't miss a beat, though, she said, 'Happy to see you' and asked after the kids. Anyway, she wanted an ordinary pair of flats, nothing special, and I went to the back room for her size. Now you won't believe this, but all the boxes on the shelves were kind of twitching, like the shoes inside were kicking to get out, or something."

He paused significantly. Molly sat across from me in mid-chew, her mouth open.

"I had to run back and forth with the ladder to push them all back in place, but they . . ."

"Frank!" Mom leaned over and shook his shoulder. Suddenly silent, he gazed at his plate and fiddled with the edge. Mom rose and took his hand and he let her lead him from the table. Molly and I were left alone with the macaroni and cheese. Mom was on the phone that night, whispering to Aunt Cissy—Dad's sister—but she fell silent whenever she heard me approach. And later, in my darkened bedroom, I created a planet where no one spoke because they were too busy thinking good thoughts.

Dad started grinding his teeth at night, producing a gnawing worse than any snore. It drove Mom to the living room couch, and it drove me there too. Finally Molly nestled among us, and we all crowded our legs and elbows as best we could. My own teeth ached from the grating that seemed to exude from the walls, and I pushed my face against the couch pillows and rustled my legs together, anything to drown it out.

"*Please,* stop it!" Mom whispered. "We don't need any more noise." So we clung to her quietly in the dark and fell asleep only from sheer exhaustion, our lullaby the crackling of molars.

When we awoke the next morning Dad was already up, buttering a piece of toast at the kitchen table. How could he have slept at all, I thought, when he was the closest to the sound of his own grinding? But what seems so strange now is that none of us mentioned our grueling night, as though Dad always gnashed his teeth and the three of us always slept together on the couch. Even Molly was unusually subdued, sipping slowly through her orange juice.

That week my body ached from sleeping each night in improvised and awkward positions, and I dreaded the sight of the afternoon shadows lengthening into the evening. One night, twisted on the couch, I dreamt that my parents were muttering to each other in a darkened room. I couldn't hear what they said, but Mom's voice sounded frightened and angry. "Please, stop it," I heard her plead. Then I was awake, afraid I had been rustling my legs again. My body was cramped against empty space, for Mom sat at the edge of the couch. Dad was bending down before her, grabbing at her feet. She kept kicking his hands away.

"What's the matter?" I asked.

Mom turned her unhappy face to me. "I don't know," she whispered, kicking her foot again at Dad's grasping hands.

"I promise you," he said, head bent, "it's a lovely shoe."

"Sammy, help me," Mom said.

Dad smiled, and I sat up terrified: he was back at his shoe store, and Mom was a customer. Now, when I think back to that night, I believe that even then I knew Dad had somehow turned himself inside out, so that the lost store he imagined surrounded us.

He edged toward me. "Welcome in! We have a sale today." I couldn't retreat: Molly was curled beside me and I didn't want to wake her. And then his hands were on my bare feet.

"Frank," Mom moaned, but he didn't listen.

"Well, sir," he said, his fingers working at my feet as if he were unlacing shoes, "I see you're a size five." I nodded. He looked up at Mom. "Madam, you have a fine boy here," and he tousled my hair. "Here's a beautiful new shoe that just came in today. Why don't we try a pair on?"

I glanced at Mom. She shook her head.

"I don't think so, thanks," I said.

He peered at me, confused and earnest. "Excuse me?" he asked.

I hesitated—I'd long wanted to be a salesman, but now that I was a customer I could finally help him make a sale. "Sure, let's try them," I said. Mom's hand was on my shoulder, and I forced myself not to look at her.

From an invisible box by his side Dad carefully lifted out an invisible shoe, and just by the way his fingers framed it I knew it would be a perfect fit. His hands slid around my foot. He held them still and I sensed his satisfaction, though this false sale saddened me. When he started to tie up the invisible laces I couldn't bear to extend the moment.

"They're great, I'll take two pairs," I said—anything to make him stand up. Mom's tight grip on my shoulder released, and I believe now that this was the moment when she no longer doubted that she had to protect her children from her husband.

She pushed him away. "That's just about enough!" she shouted, and Molly woke up. Dad struggled to his feet, his face pale and bewildered, and I doubt even now that he knew what was happening: why such anger from this oddly familiar customer? She pushed him again and Molly howled. I tugged at Mom's arm but she kept shoving him away, out the living room and down the hall. At their bedroom doorway Mom pushed him again and he fell inside, his head just missing the edge of the bedframe. We stood there at the threshold, stunned. Mom slammed the door shut.

Molly whimpered. Then we heard Dad talking in there, a kind of vigorous mumbling. His voice rose. "Steady there, steady," we could make out. "Quit it, quit that kicking." He pounded a wall.

"Don't listen," Mom said.

"Get back in the boxes!" Dad shouted. We heard him fling himself about the room and I begged Mom to open the door. She just stood there, unable to move. But when Molly rushed to the door Mom lunged at her, slapping her hands.

"Daddy, Daddeee!" Molly shrieked, and she slammed her head

against the door. Mom dragged her away and they grappled down the hall in the dark.

I was alone, listening to Dad. How easy it would be to open the door and help him, I thought, and I extended a hand. Mom called to me from the living room, "Sammy, are you still there? You mustn't listen to that!"

I hesitated. What if I opened the door and actually saw those shoes free of their boxes, tramping across the rug with a fierce anger and cornering Dad against a wall?

"Keep away, keep away!" Dad shouted from inside.

I rushed to my bedroom, where I tried to calm myself by drawing slowly on a tennis ball, hoping that carefully drawn lines would erase Dad's frightened bellowing and my vivid images of his store in revolt. A world with three continents appeared, the middle land mass the largest, and in its center was my town, and in my home Mom was opening the bedroom door. It was morning and Dad was rubbing his eyes. "What's for breakfast?" he asked. They were about to kiss, but as Mom approached she began to blur. Molly ran to them, smiling with some foolish trick that would make them laugh. Yet I couldn't imagine what it was, Molly's wailing down the hall distracted me so, and I held the tennis ball in my hand and squeezed it until the tendons in my wrist began to hurt.

It was a terrible mistake, leaving Dad alone with that invisible rebellion, and it still frightens me to think what he went through. When Mom finally opened the door we found him trembling on the carpet, and he only looked like Dad. Mom knelt down and held him with a tenderness that shocked me, and she called softly, "Frank, Frank."

The man who resembled our father almost never spoke and at dinner rarely ate. He grew thinner, looking even less familiar, and sometimes, looking at no one, his mouth moved but no sound came out. Mom made us walk barefoot, and so we moved with muffled footsteps through the house. Once Molly made a trail of silverware on the kitchen floor and she walked on it toward Dad, carefully balancing herself, bending the spoons and forks beneath her feet. But no game could make him Dad again, and while Mom scolded Molly into tears he smiled at them as if they were very far away.

When our Aunt Cissy came to visit she cried all night. Molly and I lay awake. In the sudden, brief silences we could hear Mom's tense whispering, and then Aunt Cissy started up again. I secretly hoped that if she finally stopped then Dad would be better, but I fell asleep to her sobs. The next morning Aunt Cissy put her shoes back on at the front stoop and walked to her car with a red-eyed, crushed face.

The Electric Shoe Scraper disappeared from the basement workshop soon after. The empty shoe boxes were cleared out, even the eerie circle of dust was wiped clean, and I didn't dare question Mom since I wasn't supposed to know. And then one day Dad wasn't lying as usual on the couch when Molly and I arrived home from school. Mom bustled about the kitchen, making us a snack, and I forced myself to watch her spread jam on the crackers while Molly called to Dad from room to room.

Mom stirred chocolate syrup into three tall glasses of milk and I stared at the darkening swirls chasing each other.

Molly appeared in the kitchen. "Where is he?"

"Who?" Mom said.

"I *hate* you!" Molly screamed. "Where's *Daddy?*"

"*We're* here," Mom said, her back to us, her head resting against the refrigerator, "isn't that enough?"

I left them for the worlds waiting under my bed. They lay snugly together in the cardboard box, and all of them had failed me. I took out a tennis ball and threw it against the wall. As it bounced back over my head I wondered which continent I had crushed, which happy family I had snuffed out.

That night I walked out onto the back porch with my box of tennis balls. At the edge of the lawn I picked out a thick, broken branch, and by the fluorescent light from the kitchen window I smacked one of those balls high in the air over the woods behind our yard. I watched it briefly sail off in an awkward curve before it descended into the trees, landing with a dull thud among the moist leaves on the ground. I picked up another. I slammed them again and again, listening to each one fall through the distant branches. When I was finally done I peered out into the night and realized that I couldn't let all of them go. I walked into the woods, and the branches seemed to grab at me from nowhere with gnarled and frightening fingers. I bent down to avoid them, skimming my hand across the moist dead leaves, and my hand was wet and cold when it finally gripped a round, yielding thing. This was the one I would keep. The rest could stay hidden. I worked my way back through the thicket of trees, and though the lights of my house served as a beacon, I held my little world as if I would be lost if I let go.

Our determined mother quickly earned her real estate license, with the hope that selling houses would better serve her children. Neighborhoods were rising up everywhere, transforming empty fields, and this suited Mom well because she always preferred to sell new homes. Even now, when I think of Mom I sometimes imagine her standing before a pristine and empty house, its fresh lawn dotted with the tiny shadows of newly planted saplings.

All Mom's wanting, all her fierce desires for us came true. We soon had a color TV, and when we moved to a larger house we had one for the living room and for each of our separate bedrooms. During the rare moments when we were all together in the same room Molly would suddenly clench and crackle the knuckles of her toes, which sounded so much like grinding teeth. This always drove Mom away. Then Molly nestled in her chair as if it were the lap of a parent, embracing one of the upholstered arms, a solid support that would never squirm with anger or impatience. Though I wanted to stay I followed Mom, knowing that she was alert to any sign of desertion.

I let Mom think I was who she wanted me to be, for I was all she had left. But I discovered there was an alarmingly large number of places inside myself that should be kept from her. My most hidden secret was my belief that if I closed my eyes and just walked I would be able to find Dad, no matter how far away he might be, and I often imagined myself marching down sidewalks like some clairvoyant blind child.

I actually attempted this once or twice, but with my eyes closed I could only manage a few hesitating steps, afraid that my face was about to hit a wall. How could I endure this disturbing anticipation for miles, even to find my father? And what if I did find him? Sometimes I imagined Dad alone in a little room, sitting on a cot beside a barred window, and when I entered he would look up only to see a small stranger; other times his smile of recognition would envelop me as he carefully, perfectly recounted the peculiar path that had led me to his room. *These* were the thoughts that fought inside the boy who dutifully made sure for his mother every night that all the doors and windows were locked.

I remember one evening Molly made a face out of her mashed potatoes, using broccoli as hair. "Daddy," she whispered.

"You can leave right now, young lady," Mom said, "since you can't eat food like a normal child."

Molly pushed away from the table, her face fisted up and tearless. I glanced over at her plate, at that face and the sunken sockets of its eyes. Then I grasped my knife and fork and proceeded to eat my food like a normal child, hoping that meant that I was one.

After dinner I helped with the dishes. "You're so careful, Sammy darling, even the edges are dry," Mom said, as she did every night. When I was done I went upstairs and stood in the hallway. I could see under Molly's door the television light rampaging in her darkened bedroom. I wanted to join her, but as I listened to the frenetic music and gunshots, her high laughter and the rattling of a whisk broom, I once again decided to stay a good boy.

I padded to my bedroom, where I sat among my collection of

model airplanes, my television, stereo and records and everything else I could possibly want. And through the long evening I listened to the car squeals and crashes of Molly's television coming through the walls, competing with the monotonous, canned laughter from the television Mom watched down in the living room. They slowly notched the volume up to drown each other out, and there was only one place I could escape this noise. I took out my last remaining tennis ball, closed my eyes, and imagined I was in Dad's beloved shoe store. He still worked there, business was good, and the display tables revolved so silently and slowly no one noticed. And then we were all visiting him and he wasn't shamed before us by an empty store.

We visit even now. I can't help myself, it's something I have to do whenever Mom phones me in the middle of the night, or when I realize Molly isn't going to answer my latest letter. Once again Molly and I are children, and Mom's hair is still dark and glistening. Dad's so busy he shouldn't be able to pay us any attention, but he does, with a wide grin that Mom actually returns, and their embrace is good enough to end even the longest absence. Molly and I hold on to each other and our parents, a happy knot of reconciliation, and together we stand on the smallest patch of a little world that hurtles in orbit through a clear and welcoming sky.

Angel

Bradley already knew by heart the tales of the lonely angels who hovered at busy street corners and watched careless children; of angels whose tears for all the unconfessed sins of the world created the mountain streams that emptied into the oceans; and of angels who lived in upholstered chairs and waited for lapsed believers to settle unsuspectingly into a suddenly renewed faith. Yet as he sat in the front row of the nearly empty catechism class, resisting as always the impulse to stare at the wispy hint of pompadour that dangled from Father Gregory's forehead, Bradley still listened carefully as the priest said, "Celestial beings have no bodies of their own and need none, for they are clothed in thought. But they love to assume the human form, and this they can do instantly."

The Father looked up at the ceiling, away from Bradley and the other remaining student, that young girl named Lisa who always sat in the last row. Only two left, he thought. "Some angels," he half-mumbled, "let their fingers, hands, and limbs fill out slowly, with voluptuous grace, quietly erupting from nothing into a diaphanous shape."

Though Bradley knew most of these words, he wished Father Gregory would spell the hard ones so he could look them up. But he was afraid to interrupt the Father, who, regarding his hands as if he were alone, said, "Others spend hours inventing a perfect face for their angelic temperaments." Then the Father held one hand before his lips as though suppressing a cough and continued, very softly, "There is some dispute as to whether angels invent clothes for themselves." Bradley suppressed a giggle and glanced back at Lisa. He was shocked to see her indifferent face.

At the end of all those empty rows of folding chairs, Lisa watched the Father's bulbous lips move, which she imagined slapped together. She was glad she wasn't close enough to hear, so she could decide what to make up about today's class—the last time she had told the truth about Father Gregory's stories her dad had smacked her for lying. But right now she couldn't concentrate; instead she wondered why the Father still called out the long class roll even though only two kids were left.

"It is of course well known that angels can read a person's thoughts," Father Gregory said, "but some angels will do this only briefly, for they are too easily lost within that thicket of desires and fears, strange opinions and unspoken urges—so unangel-like!" He looked down at the two students and wondered how long it would take before they too stopped coming to class, so his afternoons would finally be free. "*All* angels—the seraphim and cherubim—are addicted to us," he now whispered, "and they hover not so much to protect, but to experience us." Bradley, straining to hear this, felt uneasily that he had just heard a secret. He didn't care if he couldn't always understand; he loved being spoken to as if he were an adult.

Bradley stood beside Lisa under the church eaves and pretended, because it was raining, that his parents would be picking him up too. He wanted to ask Lisa why she kept coming to class if she didn't appreciate the Father, but she stood away from him and offered no opening for his curiosity.

Jonah and the whale, that's what we talked about, Lisa thought, watching the station wagon pull up to the curb and stop. The dim figure of her mother leaned over in the car and the window slowly slid down. "Hurry up, dear, you'll get wet," she called. Lisa's fingers scraped at her skirt. Finally, she walked to the car slowly, still not sure how long Jonah had been in that whale's stomach.

"I want to hear all about your class, sweetie," Bradley heard, and he envied such attentiveness. Then the glass rose up and the car pulled away. He remained at the church entrance and waited. His parents were probably home from work by now, and maybe one of them might actually be on the way. But the wet street was empty.

He held his school satchel over his head and walked quickly, imagining that the rain fell through his angel hovering alongside him. If only he had a bicycle. Remembering the Father's words, he tried to express himself clearly and calmly, so his angel would listen longer than usual to his unangel-like thoughts, and slowly enumerated all the special features he wanted: ten-speeds, orange-and-black trim, a bell and adjustable seat. But he wanted this bicycle only if his parents gave it to him—this would be a sign that his angel had heard.

Opening the front door, Bradley could smell dinner cooking and he walked to the kitchen. There were his parents, leaning over the stove, his father stirring a wooden spoon in the pot, his mother shaking salt into the rising steam. They stood so closely together that Bradley couldn't imagine a space for himself.

"Mom, Dad."

Jill and Bud turned to see their son standing in the doorway, holding his catechism. "Hello dear," his mother said, bending down and offering her cheek for his kiss. She rested her hand on his damp shirtsleeve. "Oh, is it raining?"

"Just a little."

Unsettled that her son had walked in the rain, Jill decided to offer Bradley his daily treat early. "Have you been a good boy today?" she asked.

Bradley nodded.

"Then here's your potato chip," she said, reaching for the counter, and she placed the chip in his waiting mouth. Her son stood still with his mouth closed, for he wasn't allowed to chew. This was their own home-grown communion: if Bradley was becoming religious, Jill couldn't see why she shouldn't exchange a greasy wafer for some quiet.

Bud said, "Well, Brad ol' boy, dinner is on the way, so why don't you take in some TV?" Bradley turned and walked down the hall to the den. Bud watched him disappear. His son's recent piety was yet another example of the inexplicability of childhood. He was pleased he could restrain himself from criticizing this latest addition to Bradley's recent manias: handwriting analysis, when his son searched the desk drawers for even the shortest note, and then that oatmeal box telephone system, with strings leading from room to room. It was so hard to be a good father in the face of such perplexing enthusiasms.

In the den, Bradley settled himself into a chair. The television was already on and waiting for him, busy with laughter and applause. Even with his eyes closed he could barely make out the indistinct murmur of his parents' voices. He wondered if their angels spoke to each other, revealing secrets about his parents that he would never know. Then he felt a salty twinge, and he concentrated on the potato chip dissolving on his tongue. Angels don't like to eat, he remembered Father Gregory once saying, because the thought of mixing food with their angelic form upsets them. But they like for us to eat, and they try to imagine taste, they try not to think of digestion. In an effort to endear himself, Bradley decided to describe his experience for his angel. First it's very salty, he thought, your tongue wants to curl up, and it's hard not to chew. When the chip starts to go mushy, you can press it—very softly—against the roof of your mouth with your tongue, and then little pieces break away. They melt very, very slowly.

Jill called her son to dinner; when he didn't answer she entered the room quietly. She regarded her son's small body, framed by the upholstered arms of the chair. His eyes were closed, and his obedient silence in front of the blaring TV was so total that he seemed about to disappear. She couldn't stop watching him, and she remembered his alarming cries as an infant, his tiny arms raised, pleading to be held.

The hardest part, Bradley thought, is to let the last piece melt instead of swallowing it. He was able to restrain himself, and soon the last bit of chip disappeared. It was terrifically difficult, he felt, to pay such close attention, and he wondered how angels could do this every instant. Suddenly his mother was before him, repeating again and again how she was going to take him to the old amusement park before it closed down. Bradley stared up at her, amazed: this wasn't a bicycle, but it was good enough.

Alone in the Ferris wheel, Bradley felt weightless circling so high up. He still didn't quite believe he was here, and the rust and the loud groans of the ancient rides couldn't spoil his pleasure. He picked at the chipped paint in his cabin, watched the little flecks flutter down, and he tried to make out his parents in the crowds below.

Jill and Bud waited below while their son spun above them. Though they had intended to come alone, Jill had managed to convince Bud to bring Bradley along. Better bumper cars and greasy food, she said, than genuflection, genuflection, genuflection. They had first met here while standing in some long line, and it was so romantic now, holding hands in this amusement park for one last time before it closed forever at the end of the season. Jill could remember Bud smiling at her in the extraordinary heat and then holding his jacket over her for a little shade.

All afternoon Bradley rode on the Loop-A-Loop, Tumble Buckets, and The Space Twister. On the boardwalk he aimed ineffectually at stacked wooden bottles, he was drawn to the pervasive promise of pizza and hot dogs wafting from the open stalls. He especially loved the sticky sweetness of cotton candy, the way it clung to the edges of his mouth and stuck to his fingers when he touched his cheek. He closed his eyes, about to describe this to his angel as a way of thanks, but then his mother bent down to wash the glistening smudges from his face.

As Bradley watched her scrape the last bit away, he heard the happy screams from the nearby roller coaster ride. He looked up at the cars making such swift, tight turns above them. Jill watched too, remembering how she'd clutched Bud's jacket on that ride so long ago.

Bud bought the tickets and fingered them with pleasure. But when they approached the seats he and Jill hesitated—the run-down roller coaster didn't fit their memories. Finally they sat together in one of the last cars, and Bradley could see that there was no room for him, although his mother patted the bit of cushion beside her. "That's okay," he said and he settled in the car behind them. The leather seat was cracked with age, and he picked at the tiny, pliable pieces while the conductor collected tickets.

The roller coaster slowly ascended the sharp rise of track with a ratchety, metallic groan. Regretting that he had ever entertained the slightest desire to be on this ride, Bradley imagined his angel was beside him. Rather than recount how the people on the ground began to shrink, however, he simply wished he had squeezed in with his parents. Bradley rattled his safety bar and hoped one of them would look back just once.

The first cars rushed down the steep slope with a curling roar and the howls of passengers. Even his parents screamed and Bradley joined in as the roller coaster hurtled to the bottom of the slope, and at each curve of track it twisted improbably one way, then another. Bradley was sure the cars would lurch from the tracks and he tightened his grip on the clattering bar. But another steep rise suddenly appeared and the roller coaster swiftly rose and fell and spurted toward another sharp turn. It tilted precipitously again, and Bradley heard a loud snap.

His parents were in the air in awkward disarray, hands clutching at their broken safety bar. They swiftly fell from sight and the roller coaster rushed down the next slope. Unable to believe what he had seen, Bradley struggled to stand in his seat, hoping his parents were somehow still in the car before him. His body trembled with the shuddering roller coaster, the wind rushed against his face and filled his open mouth, and his howls continued well past the final screeching halt at the end of the ride.

Bradley's aunt and uncle had no children after too many years of trying and they were secretly, guiltily happy to take in their favorite nephew. They fed him little treats, hoping cookies layered with tempting jams would defeat his sadness. They always made room for him on the couch, allowing any channel change he requested, and they avoided any topic concerning his mother and father.

Under the dimmed overhead lights of the dining room, Bradley watched Aunt Lena pass the cucumber salad to Uncle George while they talked of common memories that he didn't share, of neighbors he didn't know. When his uncle sipped ice water and squinted from the cold, Bradley recalled his father's features, and sometimes even his aunt's crisp footsteps to the refrigerator reminded him of his mother. Bradley stared past the chicken cutlets and wondered if his parents ever thought of him in heaven. Were their angels still with them? Bradley hated the thought that those angels, with all their memories of his parents, might be hovering next to strangers. Or did angels forget? Bradley almost envied the idea.

Though Bradley's aunt and uncle weren't religious, they remembered his parents' complaints and so they took him to church. But now he disliked having to stand and kneel all the time, and why hadn't his angel somehow warned him and his parents away from the roller coaster? While the thin priest—so unlike Father Gregory—droned the Mass, Bradley tried to recall what he could of the Father's confiding words: how angels envelop us with rapt attention; how they only want to experience us, not protect us. Bradley pictured his parents smashed on the ground, their angels hovering over them without sadness, simply satisfying their curiosity about death, while his own angel calmly examined his terrible grief.

Bradley squirmed in the pew and imagined *he* was falling through the air while his parents were safe in the roller coaster. Then, his body twisted on the pavement, dead but somehow still aware, he watched the roller coaster speed to the end. His mother and father left the ride undisturbed and walked over his body as if he weren't lying broken beneath them. They seemed like giants, and this image of his mother and father, resurrected and enormous, their indifference implacable, followed him out the church and back to his new home.

That evening he sat on the couch with his aunt and uncle in front of the television. "Tonight it's your Aunt Lena's night to choose the programs," his uncle announced with a wink. "What do you say, hon?"

She patted her nephew's knee. "I think I'm in the mood for Bradley's favorite show."

Bradley smiled up at her, sure that his angel would enjoy a description of the one-liners, even the commercial breaks, though when he turned to the television Bradley found himself once again imagining that he lay sprawled on the fairgrounds after tumbling through the sky. But this time, at his parents' approach he forced himself to rise up despite the great pain in his shattered bones. They stopped, then fled. Bradley watched their figures growing smaller and smaller, yet he felt oddly happy, for they had *seen* him. He repeated his fall, and when his parents arrived again he reached up and held their wrists. Their faces strangely impassive, they struggled until they broke away and fled again.

With each battle his parents became less substantial, and Bradley remembered that his angel must be hovering nearby, watching. Why won't it help me? he thought. Then shimmering fingers burst out of nothing and his angel reached out: slowly it loosened his grip on his straining parents until they were able to tear away. Stunned, Bradley crumpled back to the ground. His angel was a *jealous* angel and wanted no rivals.

Bradley rose from the couch, surprised to see his aunt and uncle laughing at the blaring television. "Sweetie?" his aunt began.

"I have to go to the bathroom," he said, almost running away.

He locked himself inside. It was the smallest room in the house, so small that his angel couldn't escape. "Keep away, keep away from me!" Bradley shouted, and he swung his arms wildly, hoping he struck through his angel's shape, bursting apart its invisible presence. Yet he suspected that, unlike him, it could easily heal itself, so he spun his arms about him even more and he screamed until his throat ached, his anger beyond words. His aunt and uncle pounded on the door, but he didn't let them in until he was dizzy and exhausted.

Aunt Lena held him, unable to hush his wailing, and Uncle George, alarmed at such unhappiness, reached out and awkwardly stroked his nephew's hair. "Hey, Brad ol' boy, hey Brad," he murmured.

Bradley listened to his uncle's voice, so similar to his father's, and he eased into his aunt's anxious grip. *They* wanted to comfort him, even if his angel didn't. What Father Gregory had said was true: his angel wanted only to observe him and his thoughts. Suddenly he wanted to protect his aunt and uncle from this same fearsome angel that had kept him from his parents. Remembering the intense calm he had felt when detailing the potato chip, Bradley hoped that more such careful communications might appease his angel. Slowly pushing his aunt away, he began to silently describe the crinkled look of hurt on her face.

Bradley's aunt and uncle grew accustomed to the sight of him fingering the ridges of a lampshade, the interior of a mailbox, and they were puzzled by his almost constant paging through the dic-

tionary, since he rarely spoke. Aunt Lena ached for the sound of
his voice, and whenever she touched Bradley his hesitant, endearing hug turned into a sudden breaking away, and she was left
alone in a hall, the kitchen.

One afternoon as Bradley tried to sneak outside, his aunt
called from the living room, "Where are you off to, Bradley?"

He pretended not to hear, but when he pushed open the creaking screen door she said, "Would you like a little snack first?"

"No thanks," he managed, though he was hungry.

Standing outside, he knew from the directions of the subtle,
shifting winds that a storm was approaching. All those grasping
branches above him shook and his hair swept across his forehead
like the softest of touches. He bent down and thrust his hand into
one of the last small piles of late snow. Its crystals were larger and
harder than he expected. Then he squeezed some in his fist and
felt the cold throb against his warmer skin. After the bit of snow
dissolved, Bradley slowly swept his tongue over the lines of his
palm, silently describing each ticklish ripple. The rain began to
fall. Bradley stood there as it soaked his hair and drained down his
face, its taste vaguely metallic against his parted lips, and he
recorded scrupulously how his increasingly wet clothes matted
against him, how an oddly pleasurable chill spread over his body.

Aunt Lena dropped the cauliflower she was washing in the sink
when she glanced out the window and saw Bradley standing
drenched in the middle of the backyard, his face turned up into
the rain. She ran outside, wailing his name.

That night Lena and her husband sat beside Bradley's bed,
alarmed at their feverish nephew's smile while he touched his
forehead carefully with his fingers, as if for the first time. When
Bradley recovered three days later, Uncle George bought him a
bicycle. They sat together in the driveway and attached baseball
cards to the spokes for an intricate, ratchety sound, and Uncle
George patiently ignored those unnerving moments when his
nephew sat still, his eyes distant, his hands working at nothing.

But Bradley was rarely at home. Instead he ranged through the neighborhood, discovering the patterned silences between bird calls, the new green shoots and their clusters of buds within buds. Dizzy and oppressed by the seemingly endless supply of the world, he doubted he could ever chronicle it all for his angel, and one evening, while listening to his uncle's faraway voice calling him, Bradley stood transfixed beneath an evergreen tree lit by a street lamp. In the odd light its needles were an unearthly green. Detailing the ascending, branched pattern of the thin needles, which resembled an odd spiral staircase, he realized that the convoluted spaces between the branches were passages for the wind. But he could only see these spaces by looking at the branches, which in turn held no pattern without the surrounding emptiness, and Bradley was reminded of his own invisible, complementary presence.

After years of plumbing the hidden corners of dictionaries, words had become for Bradley exquisite bearers of comfort, yet by high school the frequent sight of boys and girls necking furtively in the school hallways filled him with a strange longing for which there were no words. He found brief solace in gym class, deftly kicking a soccer ball that seemed to float endlessly in the air before suddenly eluding the goalie, or exulting in a basketball's intricate, rhythmic music as he sped down the court.

Despite his sometimes unnerving solitude a few girls thought he was cute; Debby Wickers, who seemed to always appear by his hall locker, adjusting the pile of books under her arm, thought he was handsome. But after so often standing near his locker with nothing to say or do, Debby was almost ready to give up on Bradley ever acknowledging her.

One day Bradley was pressing his hands against the side of his locker door, mutely describing the touch of metal and how its edges are almost sharp enough to cut—anything to avoid facing the girl who always stood so close to him, to suppress his curiosity about her constancy. But when he heard the sound of her patient sigh, there was something final in it that made Bradley turn and look at her steady dark eyes, her thick brown hair. "What's your name?" he asked, so quietly, and Debby felt he was staring at her face as if he were trying to memorize it.

The next evening he was at Debby's house, helping her with algebra. They sat on the carpet in her room, books open and paper scattered, while her parents called up regularly to ask how their homework was coming along. Bradley stammered out the solutions to the problems, and Debby was pleased—his nervousness was so flattering. When she had enough of answers she already knew, she stretched out on the floor, yawned, and then glanced up at Bradley. The night before she had made a long-distance call to her sister in college. "Let him take off just one thing," her sister had said. "He'll be chained to you after that, he'll want to know what's under the rest of your clothes." Debby put her hand on his knee and smiled before she turned away.

Bradley wanted to touch the back of her neck where her dark hair seemed to burst out of nowhere, but he was at the center of an invisible stage, his curious angel the audience. Debby looked over her shoulder and reached for Bradley. Though he knew he shouldn't touch her, he tried to convince himself that her beckoning hand had just waved his angel away. He tentatively stroked her wrist and she snuggled against him. Instead of pushing her away, he gently touched Debby's neck and she arched her back. After a long moment he finally cupped his hand and slowly placed it over a breast, the cloth of her blouse softly tickling his palm.

Bradley let Debby lead his hands to one button after another until the thought of his angel, capable of anything, returned. Debby saw his face blank over. Shocked that he was resisting what she offered, she coaxed him into unfastening her belt, and before long she forgot everything her sister had advised.

When Debby was finally, stunningly exposed beside him, Bradley felt the habitual urge to describe what he saw. *Never* any privacy, *never* alone? he thought. He closed his eyes, refusing to explicate Debby, but already he could sense the presence of an angry, invisible hand. "No!" Bradley shouted, "No!" Debby sat up, frightened by Bradley's cries, by the sound of steps up the stairs. The door to her room opened. Debby held her skirt against her, but she could tell from her father's brief, horrified glance that he could see right through it. And then he was after Bradley, who was still shouting, his eyes still closed.

In college Bradley majored in Accounting and immersed himself in long spreadsheets, half hoping that his angel would eventually grow bored by the regularity of numbers. But that intimate presence had become a habit he couldn't cast out; Bradley sometimes wondered if Father Gregory had felt this way. He tried to remember the Father's long-ago words but could only see his lips moving: a silent, distant performance.

He always sat by himself in the dormitory dining hall, tired from programming long columns of audits and inventories, and though he was proud of his secret eloquence, Bradley listened with envy to the chaotic accumulation of speech and laughter that rose and fell in the large hall. He understood grimly that he had forgotten how to talk to other people, and he tried to imagine how his voice might sound as part of those alien give-and-take rhythms. But he spoke directly to no one, for he was afraid *not* to believe in his angel's possessive will, and when he felt words brimming up he panicked: he released them as sudden laughter, great huffing gulps of sound that held no happiness.

Soon Bradley couldn't stop these cheerless bursts, and he began to haunt the local comedy club whenever he felt the need to speak. Sitting alone at the bar, he held back a welter of words and hoped his awkward laughter blended in with the hearty convulsions of the strangers around him. He stared at the rows of bottles lined up beneath the mirror, those almost transparent bodies filled with clear or strangely colored liquids: how he envied the way they could be so easily emptied.

One night he arrived for the Open Mike Spotlight, the least

entertaining show of the week, and he had to endure long stretches before he could join in with any appreciative guffaws and snorts. Yet he couldn't stop watching the painfully amateur failures who grasped at even the most modest reward from the audience. That night's barmaid, frightened by his desolate laughter, considered refusing him another beer—whatever tormented the poor guy, no drink would drown it.

Finally, after a middle-aged man's ten-minute repertoire of personal noises, the MC announced "Last call." Bradley finished his beer, edged off his stool, and was alarmed to discover he was walking toward the stage. He wanted to stop, but he felt the same as when that roller coaster had started its slow climb and there was no turning back. He stepped into the spotlight, absolutely uncertain of himself. As he adjusted the mike he listened to the loud, amplified crunks, the murmur of distant and unfamiliar voices. They were waiting, listening, and Bradley remembered his parents' funeral, when he had been the mute center of everyone's attention. His throat constricted—if he didn't speak right now he might never speak again. A few people in the audience began to applaud ironically.

"Better be careful," Bradley heard himself say, "God doesn't like irony." Where is *this* coming from? he thought, but more words rose up and he released them. "Irony introduces ambiguity, which undermines the power of God's Word, and His punishment is the Angel of Irony."

There were a few hoots, and the MC began to edge toward the stage. They think I'm a fanatic, a crank, Bradley realized with alarm. "No, wait," he said, "I'm only trying to be helpful. You see, the Angel of Irony is drawn to irony but, ironically enough, can't understand it. Maybe one day that angel will float nearby when you say something like, 'It sure would be great to live in this little dump for the rest of my life.' Then it'll grant you your wish and you'll be stuck in that dump no matter what you try to do."

Bradley paused, struck by the fluidity of his strange thoughts and the booming sound of his amplified voice. He looked out at the audience, their faces pale disks in the dark. Were they waiting for a punch line? He had none, so he plunged on.

"And what about your personal angel? There's one sitting right beside you now and yet somehow taking up no space at all. Since an angel has no substantial presence it can compress itself to the size of a synapse, can follow the extraordinarily swift and winding ways of a thought. But it must have *some* weight: imagine that this extra bit of almost nothing attaches to a memory or the beginning of a thought and subtly alters its forward motion, veering it, however slightly, to another neuron. Could our daily indecisions," he continued, exhilarated, "be the contrast between what we truly want and where our concentrated knot of angel has taken us? Maybe we're compositions, evolving works of art for angels, and they're attracted to the elegant patterns they make of our fates."

The audience was terribly quiet, but Bradley felt more words forming and he could hold nothing back. "It's late. Maybe you'd like to leave, right now, and get away from all my idiotic words, but your angel swerves you away from such a thought. Your angel is vain. Trained by a life of eavesdropping, it can't resist listening to such delicious talk. And maybe it's anticipating the pleasure, when everyone applauds, of its transparent body fluttering in the small explosions of the surrounding air."

Finally emptied, Bradley felt almost weightless, actually released from that burrowing presence, and this purging was pleasurable, a loss that was simultaneously gain. But then the oppressive need to describe returned, and he couldn't help listening carefully to the applause, that indecisive clapping of hands that was both restrained and enthusiastic, conveying at the same time curiosity, appreciation, and resistance.

Although no one could really call his monologues comedy, Bradley became a regular at the club, and soon he was known informally as the Angel Man. Ignoring the clink of glasses, the whoosh of the tap at the bar, he held on to the microphone stand as if it tethered him to the stage, and the intensity of his concentration quieted the occasional heckler. He was immediately filled with words that metamorphosed into phrases and sentences, hungry for that exhausted moment after a performance when, briefly emptied of his angel, he had to clutch the plush curtain backstage and ease into its swaying.

But often his eloquence didn't seem his own, and Bradley suspected that his angel was confessing its inexplicable qualities. "Consider this," Bradley found himself saying one evening, "since an angel has no voice, it assumes the vocal inflections of its human companion, and what we sometimes believe to be private thoughts are actually communications from our angels." Yet as he listened to himself—or was it to his angel?—Bradley wondered if he might be able to pour out all those words inside until they couldn't be replenished, if one night he might finally be deserted.

He returned to the club as often as possible, pushing his impromptu inventions and never repeating himself. "Imagine how different angels are from us," he said one evening, "because what we can't do without, angels don't need: food, clothes, houses, doorways, or cars. . . ." For one dizzy moment Bradley had nothing to say, and he was filled with a wild thought: Could this really be the last emptying?

Bradley closed his eyes, and in the dark he briefly created he saw a young girl's face appear, a dot of memory he immediately knew belonged to Lisa, that girl who sat in the back during catechism class. She regarded Bradley with total disinterest, and then her features altered and multiplied into his mother's and father's, both imperturbably facing him. He reached out to prevent their escape, but there were no wrists to grasp.

Hearing nervous coughs, Bradley opened his eyes and simply stood there, searching foolishly through the audience for his parents' faces. Then he noticed a young couple sitting at a front table: the man smiled a steady, peculiar smile, but it was the woman's impassive gaze, which seemed not to see Bradley at all, that drew him. He needed to speak to her, only to her, and at once he felt a great stillness inside him.

"Imagine a being who shares your secrets," he began, leaning forward on the stage, "the ones you manage to conceal from everyone. Compared to your angel, your intimacy with your spouse is similar to your occasional dealings with a salesclerk. Are you here tonight with a husband, a wife? Look at that stranger beside you, so unable to challenge the secret knowledge of your angel."

Diane didn't dare glance over at her relentlessly devout husband who had come here just because he loved to be appalled. All evening she'd had to pretend she was bored, but now the Angel Man seemed to speak directly to her, and Diane was afraid he saw past her false face and knew how stunned she was by his words.

"Remember, to angels we are both storm and ballast," Bradley said, anxious for even the barest flicker of interest on the woman's face. "We're a promising harbor for an angelic grip, but we are also the most turbulent of passages, the tightest of squeezes for an angel once it truly wants to slip inside us."

Diane watched the Angel Man, his face so peaceful in the spotlight. She thought of her husband's angel: twisted in his heart, its wings crushed and worthless, its sad contortions resembling his fist on the table. She could sense him stirring angrily in his seat, aware of the attention she was receiving. She dreaded going home, where she was helpless before the unyielding injustice of his opinions, where even her dreams couldn't escape the sound of his angry voice. She kept her face a blank.

"We're sometimes too voluminously primitive," Bradley continued, "a catalogue of imperfections, for angels to truly enjoy us. I sometimes wonder why angels hover beside us if we're such an inexpressibly crude version of themselves, for they have more facets than we can imagine, each one lit by a light we can't see. Perhaps our angels are prodigiously unfaithful and temporarily leave us, from boredom or exhaustion, to enter the mind of a new and excitingly unfamiliar human. Perhaps my own angel has done this. Perhaps it will someday leave me forever for someone new."

He stopped and stared at the woman's stiff face. She isn't even listening, he thought, at best she's holding back a yawn. He looked out over the rest of the faces in the audience, but they all seemed to recede from him.

Diane imagined his angel speeding toward her, whispering the sorts of secrets she had listened to all evening. The lone spotlight dimmed and she could just make out, "Whoever receives my angel, you're welcome to every dogged attention it's capable of, and may it give you better fortune than it ever gave me." She looked up in gratitude, but the Angel Man had turned his back on her and the rest of the audience. As he walked offstage, Diane felt dangerously, deliciously weightless, and her lips tingled with forbidden words. And what *could* her husband do, she thought, if her words were not her own, how could he possibly reply if she howled out at him in an angelic rage? Already she saw him openmouthed and speechless before her.

Bradley stopped backstage, giddily empty, and he clung to the heavy folds of the curtain. He kept repeating to himself those last words, hoping to stave off his angel's possible return. Through the curtain he could hear the rasp of chairs pushing back, murmuring voices, footsteps. He envied that crowd out there, leaving to return to their own lives. Then he thought, I'm the only life my angel has. And this seemed to be its own strange comfort, one that might forever help him to endure his companionable loneliness. But this insinuating idea also alarmed Bradley, and he checked an urge to describe the dark curtain, even though it shimmered along its length from his slightest touch.

Interior Design

These days I just won't get out of bed, so I lie here, idly kicking the sheets into strange patterns—a ripple of dunes, a mountain range—and I imagine I'm a peasant woman in Turkey, working alongside her husband, carving out a home from one of those cliffs of soft volcanic rock. I can see our faces and hands dusty and smeared with stone shavings and sweat, two strange creatures chipping away new rooms as we need them, and I wonder if we'll agree on every odd turning we take in the rock, every little nook or window we each wish.

All my life I've longed for something like this with a gnawing eagerness: to live among the eighty percent of the world's people who build their own homes. Unfortunately, I belong to that remaining, privileged minority: the suburbanites, who make themselves content in their cozy cubes with a narrow hall or a window's unwanted view; and the apartment dwellers, who live in rooms silently echoing with the habits of former tenants. So as an interior designer I always saw myself as a medium, helping my clients discover the house they wanted to have in the house where they already lived. I wanted to be invisible, to interfere as little as possible with my clients' desires, working within the constraints of their imaginations and the building code.

I asked, "Where would you really like to live?" and I listened to their idiosyncratic, secret dreams of home. Together we created an interior as familiar as the self, made the walls as comfortable as skin: I simply settled into someone else's mind and gave it doors and windows. There was always an urgency to my work, because I believed there's an ideal home inside each of us that slowly shrinks unless it's found.

I did my first work in the heartland, for people living in small towns who wanted their homes to counter the vast, flat spaces around them. My first clients were an elderly couple who imagined something they called Polynesian Splendor: vistas of golden beach, palm fronds, and clear tidal pools. What could be better than a home that was also a vacation, a prison that was its own parole? And that's what I gave them, though the details had to be mundane as well as exotic, because I knew these folks weren't going to leave, they just wished they could. I decided to work with local products and craftspeople: plastic palm trees from K Mart, quarry sand for the back porch. The mural painted over the indoor pool was inspired by a cheesy Dorothy Lamour movie poster, yet I made sure touches of phosphorescent paint were applied here and there, so that in the dark those tropical stars would shine, those shells glint.

Soon, the aspiring displaced sought me out, and dotted throughout miles and miles of fields were private escapes hidden in ordinary houses: two unmarried sisters and their series of indoor fountains commemorating a trip to Old Faithful; or a widower who turned the tower of his three-story Victorian into a lighthouse and cast nightly beams across his fields, where the shadows of corn stubble could have been anything. With all my clients I worked on the cheap, I even gave discounts, because I didn't want to make too much money, I wanted to work off my father's sins.

I remember him returning home in the evenings, taking off his coat with great deliberation, and regarding me and my two younger sisters as if we were carpet stains that Mother hadn't cleaned up yet. He barely had to speak to remind us we were failures for not having been born boys and that Mother was the failure who produced us.

"Hello Phyl," he said to Phyllis, who nodded.

"Hello Pat," he said to Patricia, who smiled her guilty smile.

"Hello, Jo," he said, looking at me.

"Josephine," I always corrected him.

My father was a house builder, and his office was a demonstration home where the furniture displayed in all the rooms was three-quarter sized. The smaller the furniture, he slyly reasoned, the larger the rooms looked, so when potential customers walked casually through his demonstration home they believed they were in much fuller spaces. I thought this was a terrible way to make a living, to ensure that a home grew smaller once a family moved in with their full-sized furniture. Think of it, an entire house a subtle, secret lie! Their walls static but always closing in, the family would become increasingly irritable and argue over nothing. Throughout my childhood I wanted my father to be a fireman, someone who *saved* homes.

We moved from place to place before Father's dissatisfied customers could accumulate, and over the years he filled our successive homes with three-quarter-sized cast-offs from his old displays. Each chair and table was a hard example of his special talent for belittling those around him. My mother was already shrunken under his steady contempt and Phyllis and Patricia, with their carefully imposed silences, were ripe for squeezing themselves into reduced limits. My sisters fit so well that Father soon took them along to work on weekends, where they became part of his devious display and helped his sales. I was never invited to the showroom because, happily, I was too tall for my age.

I grew up frightened by and yet longing for furniture. A simple chair with its inviting cushions was a forbidding object, and when I thought of my mother and sisters forever crimped, I was prepared for the discomfort of fitting nowhere in our home. I remember at dinnertime looking at all the plates and glasses, obscenely huge on the runty table, and I insisted on sitting on a telephone book. "It's for my posture," I explained, though my secret reason was I didn't want to touch that chair, and because I never leaned back—to avoid resting against the tiny wicker backing—I endured those childhood dinners with aching shoulders.

My willful isolation from the contamination of touch also extended to my mother and sisters: I couldn't bear the thought of a stunted embrace. So it was a thrilling release to hear, however cautious and clinical the telling in my school's sex education class, about the grapplings of love. I was proud to discover how girls were much more complicated than boys, that women were born with their ovaries full, an egg waiting decades to be fertilized by a single shrimp of a sperm. My opinion of Father lowered still further for his inability to appreciate us, and then I learned it was the male who determines the sex of the child.

I took no small pleasure in telling my father that *he* was the failure of the family. "I don't need to hear such language from *you*, young lady," he said.

Mother sat across from us, her eyes made dull by patience. Yet there was a minute smile on her face—a smile that I would see at the oddest moments for the rest of my life—and I wondered, was it faint support, or relief that she was momentarily forgotten?

"That's right," I laughed, "I *am* a young lady, not a stupid son."

"Don't you talk to me that way," Father shouted, "you sit down here and . . ."

"In this creepy furniture? Forget it." While Father sputtered, my sisters huddled beside their dollhouse: prisoners playing a game of Warden, poking their dolls into furniture even smaller than ours. And then I remembered something else from biology class, about age and the atrophy of bones. I shouted at Father that like everyone else he was going to shrink with old age and die three-quarter sized on a full-sized bed. He stood there silent and trembling, with a face so fallen I ran from the room, furious that my father wasn't as untouchable as I had imagined. That night, and for long after, I dreamt *I* was three-quarter sized: my legs, arms, head and heart, and I was crammed inside that damned dollhouse. My body was bent and buckled, an arm out a window, a leg down a stairwell, and then I reversed and grew so small I could fit in one of those rooms, sitting comfortably on a tiny couch, staring at the blank screen of the plastic television.

Years later, the hardest part of architecture school for me was making models. Whenever I resisted realizing my vision of a building with a miniature version, I discovered that my professors had their own version of my father's frown and they lectured with his voice. But I had long been adept at defying the local measurements, and anyway I found myself more and more attracted to interior design. I devoured every book I could find on any sort of home—nothing could be too exotic—and when I discovered that in Indian longhouses even the placement of the most humble hammock is charged with mystical purpose, I knew that I wouldn't be satisfied with just drywall and doorways, plumbing and thermal units.

When those first interior design projects of mine landed me a ten-page color spread in *Plains Living*, I received enthusiastic calls from both coasts. I decided to go East—I didn't like the idea of any earthquake leveling my best efforts, since my father was still selling his houses somewhere and I felt I had a lot of catching up to do. Now, lying here stretched out on my bed, I think, What's so bad about earthquakes? and I pound my arms and legs against the mattress to make even the pillows shake.

But at the time I thought I'd hit pay dirt, since all my new clients could much better afford to reproduce their desires for comfort. There were the sociology professors Jack and Maxine, who were cashing in on the third and final edition of their once popular textbook, *Class Marx*. "We're the last bastion, and we want no false consciousness in our house," Jack said, and Maxine continued, "Jack and I are noted for the theory that walls were the first form of social obfuscation." And so they asked for glass panes on the walls to reveal the electrical wiring and the heating ducts, a porthole in the hallway overlooking their bed, even a stained-glass panel on the bathroom door. They requested Lucite steps for the stairway to the second floor, in order to expose those stairs directly beneath that led to the basement. "Get it?" Jack beamed, looking down. "It's a critique of the myth of social mobility!"

Another client lavished a fortune on redesigning his apartment after the recent deaths of his three dearest friends. A quiet, alarmingly thin man who liked to crumple cellophane wrappers and paper cups while he talked, during our first consultation he said, "I dream that I'm walking along these rained-out gullies and crevices and it's funny, I wake up crying but I feel relieved." He wanted his apartment to resemble erosion: the corners of baseboards split apart, a comforting wall of rubble, bookshelves artfully eaten away as if by termites, lampshades carefully ripped to create disjunct slashes of light. All this static decay both commemorated his losses and hinted at an end to them, just as he hoped his own disease would stop at a certain point and go no further.

Almost every one of my projects became a magazine spread, and I was much in demand. But in all of these homes I was a stranger—I helped my clients find their comfort yet it was never mine. Attempting to save others, I began to suspect, was not the same as saving oneself. Something in me still distrusted furniture, as if my father were a noxious, invisible wallpaper waiting to clash with whatever interior I might choose for myself. So I lived in a studio apartment with the barest of essentials—table, chair, bed—that would confound even my conforming sisters, and I was resigned to this spartan shelter because of my recurring dream.

In this dream I was always floating in a vast and empty darkness, my body flat as if lying on my back. I'd been floating for quite a long time, it seemed, and as I drifted aimlessly through this absence of architecture I wondered what patterns my body made, what involuntary dance I was creating. The longer I levitated, like some buoyant vagabond, the more I began to suspect that this floating endlessly was my own form of oblivion. But whatever my fears, I continued to drift.

That strange, characterless space seemed to accompany me through the day, seeping into my thoughts at any moment. Why not define that emptiness, I asked myself, why not design my own dream? I began a little game of mentally collecting furniture, imagining that each piece patiently anticipated a release inside me, just like eggs in the ovaries. I produced a Louis Quinze chaise voyeuse to sit on as I floated, I materialized a hovering halogen lamp, though its small circle of light couldn't possibly penetrate the vast darkness. I felt like my sisters playing with their dollhouse, trying to do their best with the space given them, though instead of tiny walls I had an infinite layout, and I conjured up arrangements until I had not a room but an entire home spread out in that nothingness.

It was those private designs that led me to the secret history of objects: they're all the products of desire. The first chair didn't just appear like some mushroom rising out of the floor. Instead, long ago someone, somewhere, thought, "I'm tired," and only then was a chair built, its wooden existence fitting the need. In the same way, the thought, "I'm cold," conceived walls and a roof. We actually turn ourselves inside out and find comfort in what we've imagined. If the guitar, the violin, the piano are extensions of us, created to give voice to our longings, then furniture is no less musical, though its song is silent. Lounging on a divan in my dreamy home, I realized that if every object around us is a bit of mind, made material, then my father was guilty of lobotomizing the homes of his clients.

But with that thought my mother suddenly appeared from behind a wardrobe with her ambiguous smile. Then Phyllis and

Patricia arrived, their shoulders hunched as they tried out a bar stool, a rocker, which seemed to shrink at their touch. And when I heard my father's thick footsteps—on *what,* in that void?—I let everything vanish and I was back to floating, safe once again.

And then I met Frederick. When I entered his office he was jotting down a note, perched on the edge of his seat: his body cantilevered over the desk and casually defying gravity, the fingers of one hand holding him steady while he wrote with the other. I wanted to see how he'd keep that up—observing my clients' relationships to their furniture was always important to me—so when he glanced up and said, "Sorry, just one moment," I quickly replied, "Please, don't let me disturb you," and I marched over to a chair.

I looked around: the typical investment counselor's office, computer terminals and telephones the dominant features. On the shelf was a photo of him and a beautiful woman who was obviously a wife, and I was oddly pleased to see there were no children. She was short, about three-quarters of his height, I couldn't help thinking. How tall *is* he? I wondered, wishing I'd let him stand up, but he was still precariously balanced and scribbling away. Here's a man on the edge, I thought, and I didn't mind admitting to myself I was right when he finally put down the phone, sat back, and immediately announced he'd just been divorced. I couldn't help gaping at the photograph—how sweet that he still kept it—and he caught me and glanced over too, a furtive, lingering look. I sympathized, knowing what it was like to be gripped by the insistent past, and I thought he was touchingly hesitant when he said, "I have a new house. It's small, but elegant, and . . . uh, empty. I'm living out of an apartment now. Is it true, from what I've heard of your work, that I'll have to dream up this new home of mine?"

I started in with my usual speech about personal, continuing environments. Frederick nodded, taking a note or two, and he seemed so alone behind his desk, so abandoned. Suddenly I couldn't concentrate: my secret cache of furniture was emptying itself inside me. A Philippe Stark table, a Bank of England swivel chair, octagonal marble tiles, an Alsatian blanket chest and more tumbled out into empty vistas, impeding the responses I made to Frederick's questions, though he didn't seem to notice. Oh god, I thought, what'll I do when my family starts to climb over this jumble? He rose, thankfully, before those apparitions could arrive and he said, "I really think we can work together." We shook hands, and somehow I was able to notice we were the same height, a perfect match.

But we couldn't begin designing his house because his imagination locked up. All day he carried a blank notepad, unable to snatch a stray idea. Each morning he woke with a vision of nothing, and though he tried setting his alarm randomly for different times in the night, he was never able to snare a single dream. In our meetings in his office he recounted these difficulties in a very businesslike manner, almost as if I were taking dictation, while he tried to avoid glancing over at that damn photo on his shelf.

In an effort to unblock him, we agreed on a tour of his new house. We walked through his echoing rooms, all that bare space so fraught with possibility, yet nothing came to him. "What do *you* dream?" he finally asked me in frustration. I stood there, stirred up by the seductive tensility of the empty room, and I told him about that vast, dreamy void I floated in at night, and as he listened I was suddenly certain about the cause of his trouble: in his mind he was still married to his ex-wife. She was haunting his new house, occupying space that just wasn't hers, and I decided right there to become a homewrecker: how else could Frederick's house become his own unless I chased her away?

I leaned a little too close to him. "It's warm in here," I said, and I started taking off my sweater. I could feel it pull my blouse up a bit, exposing my navel, a little circle of darkness to set him off. Frederick reached over for me, and when his hand circled my own I knew he could do whatever he wished.

Afterward, I lay on my back beside him on the hard wooden floor. His hand played with me lazily and I kept dripping: already we were marking our territory. "Tell me that dream again," he whispered. Lying there, I felt as if I *were* floating, and as I spoke I imagined Frederick above me again, my eyes scanning his face and the ceiling, and then I knew what could be done for the lighting in the room: bury the lights in the ceiling and space them to echo the traffic pattern below, so they could be turned on and off by passing feet. I saw us walking through the room, creating a path of light.

We moved into Frederick's empty house, intending to design rooms as we needed them. It was the first time I allowed myself to gather in the hidden signals, and my mind was inflamed with possible order. And although Frederick was still blocked, there was something about his helplessness before an empty space that drove me wild. So *I* began to fill up the house. Every idea I suggested delighted him, and he said, "That's fine, let's try it," as if our intuitions were identical.

I wanted our bedroom to be my dream, or *our* dream, since Frederick had adopted it. I wanted us to feel we were floating in the air. I took out the windows and replaced them with glass bricks, the thick panes filtering in a hazy, self-contained light like no other. All the walls and the ceiling were painted sky blue, though scumbled in places with white powder for a hint of cirrus, and in one corner the blue gradually deepened to navy—acknowledging the possibility of storm, but easily confining it. Above the turquoise carpeting all the furniture was white—the two wardrobes, the night tables, and the bedframe that seemed to hover on its thin legs—and every edge was rounded, like a solid ooze of cloud. Against the white headboard nestled blue pillows over a white quilt, which in turn covered blue sheets, so when we clambered over each other in bed we kicked up a convulsion of sky and cloud. *We* were the moving parts that made the house breathe and change.

So I finally allowed myself to empty my inner warehouse. I purposely cluttered every room with furniture of all varieties and epochs, a style I secretly titled Cornucopia. I gave in to the warmth of wood, the fluted metal edges of high tech, the plush comfort of a velvet seat, and the laying out of plans gave me a sexual pleasure, each arrangement an inducement to a tryst. On the walls I hung up paintings, prints, and photographs of furniture and nothing else, echoing that flood of furniture when I first met Frederick. I matted and framed them at slight, odd angles that only the most acute eye would unambiguously notice. I liked the tension of the pictures firmly on the walls and yet seeming only momentarily suspended, as though they were about to float down and take their places in the rooms.

This sense of expectancy reminded me of the women in India who daily decorate the earth in front of their houses with elaborate designs of rice powder, the interwoven lines being offerings to the gods. I thought colored chalk would do nicely for our house, though a drawing a day was too much. I had no gods to propitiate, I simply wanted to exemplify the shifting moods of our house, and only when one pattern wore off or was rained away would I start another. Once I began an elaborate motif of numbers—large and small, in every possible color—to influence Frederick's fortune into a limitless success. He tried to help and we knelt on the porch together, our hands dirty with colored chalk. Frederick grew annoyed with himself for his awkward sketching, which he couldn't improve despite my helpful hints. Eventually I eased him out of sight of the street and we smeared each other's faces with our chalky hands until we were harlequin twins, our improvised masks making us familiar strangers, and we made a ferocious, technicolor love.

Blissfully domestic, all day I transformed the house into a dream-scape we could walk through wide awake, and in the evenings I waited for my man to come home and be amazed. But I worried about Frederick. He had stopped trying to remember his dreams. I couldn't understand it—in certain areas he suffered no lack of invention. I was afraid he might resent my success at filling empty spaces, so I kept trying to goad his imagination.

It was October and I had just sketched a giant stadium on the porch, with baseballs flying out—all of them homers for our team. While we watched the Series, a huge bowl of popcorn between us, I said casually, "Hon, did you know there's a country where hosts polish their chairs incredibly carefully, so when a visitor sits on one its smoothness rubs off and makes him a good guest?"

"Shhh," he said, "a three and two pitch."

I waited until the strikeout before trying again. "Y'know," I said, stretching back a little, hoping he'd glance at me, "I read somewhere there are people in Africa who believe your soul lives in your chair. No one else can sit there. And when you're not sitting on the chair you tip it over. So your soul can't be stolen."

Frederick kept his mouth stuffed with popcorn so he wouldn't have to answer. I knew he was annoyed, but I couldn't help myself, I flicked off the game with the remote control.

"Imagine that," I said, "a chair isn't just a chair, it's what people *think* a chair is."

He grabbed the control away from me and mumbled through his popcorn, "Well, that's certainly *one* way to look at it."

That stopped me. I always told him there were many ways to see something, but it was true that I wanted him to see it *my* way. He knew the contradiction I was caught in. He flipped a kernel in the air and caught it in his mouth, enjoying my discomfort.

All those happy rooms in the house slowly transformed into traps with invisible springs, waiting to be set off by my reproachful suggestions and Frederick's sullen resentment. He didn't want to be a disappointment, so he was trying to make me one. I thought of my mother, enduring too much contradiction with her slight smile that was impossible to read. I wouldn't let *that* happen to me. I fought back.

So we argued over even the silliest things. And then came that evening when, while washing dishes—though I suspected it wasn't my turn—I told Frederick how my father blamed my mother for having girls. Suddenly, incredibly, we were disagreeing over what men and women were most like, the letter Y or the letter X! This was somehow connected with the X and Y chromosomes, though at that point we could have argued over the letters G and K. "C'mon, people are like the Y," he said, sitting restlessly at the kitchen table. "When we're born, we don't know what sex is, and we grow up together through childhood like the base of the Y. But look, at puberty we become different and split off, we move farther apart the older we get." His feet tapped at the floor tiles in a most annoying fashion.

"No, no, no," I said, "you're all wrong, we're like the X. Our sex makes us different right from the start, so we're like the opposite bottom legs of the X. But that difference attracts us, and when we make love, we're joined together in the middle. Then we move apart until we make love again."

He wouldn't agree. I hated that—I wanted us to be the same letter, and though the X and Y are right next to each other in the alphabet it was no consolation. "X, X, X!" I screamed at him, red-faced like a child, and I slapped a sponge and soap bar into the dishwater, just for emphasis. I had come to that. Frederick stood up, and his look of contempt forced me to slam the kitchen cabinets. I thrilled to the sound of the spaghetti and cereal boxes shuddering inside. Frederick almost spoke, but then he turned to leave, tripping over his chair. He gasped and they both tumbled down.

I stood at the sink and watched him lying there beside the overturned chair: I waited for him to give it a good kick, to shout at it, to smash it in anger. But he simply rubbed his shoulder. I kept waiting, until he began to pull himself up. Then I rushed over and we made our usual, insufficient apologies, enough to last us another evening.

Later that night, after a half hour of ineffectual clutching, we turned out the bedroom lights and I felt that the ominous patch of navy blue I'd consigned to one corner had grown into the surrounding dark. I lay there listening to Frederick's satisfied breathing. I tried so hard to imagine his hand rising to strike the chair, but his fist kept dissolving into the air until I finally fell asleep.

The next morning I woke in bed alone—Frederick had already left for the office. Furious at him for sneaking off like that, I kicked away at the clinging sheets, felt the satisfaction of my anger releasing, and then I understood how terribly dead Frederick's world must be. He didn't assume in his deepest self that a chair was somehow alive and could be hurt. Punching it was a childish but endearing form of revenge he was incapable of pursuing, and what I had thought were just contrary arguments were actually his most personal way of seeing. The true essence of our house had escaped him: for Frederick, furniture was just furniture.

Then everything in the room became dead for me as well and shed its invisible skin: the carpet was mere tufted wool, the bedframe only painted pine, the blue walls an ordinary acrylic blend. And though this lasted only a few seconds, it was unbearable. I closed my eyes and when I opened them I was once again surrounded by resonant expanses of blue and white. But I was no longer floating. I was falling, and I didn't know where I'd land.

I couldn't see Frederick again. I was afraid he would infect me with that hidden deadness of objects. Worst of all, I realized I had done something I'd tried to avoid all my life: I had imposed an interior. I had forced Frederick to live with an alien vision and I actually hoped he would eventually tear it all down, though what he tore down would be me. Everything ends, I thought bitterly, even houses collapse. I fingered the white quilt and remembered my teenage days of sexual discovery in a thick woods, romping on a leafy bed among empty beer cans and old condoms within a scattered stone foundation—all that was left of an abandoned house. In a way, those exuberant scramblings had briefly made it a home again. Would young kids someday find a haven here?

I knew I had to leave, though I was everywhere in that house. I knocked over all the furniture so my soul couldn't be stolen, but I was afraid that when Frederick returned he might simply set it all upright again, merely perplexed and angry. So before I left I crawled about the porch and drew my face again and again: in sorrow, pain, anger, reproach, and fear, each face partially superimposed on the other like a chain of dismaying portraits before his doorstep. I imagined him arriving home and, seeing what I'd drawn, know instantly that I'd left. I wanted him distraught, unaware he was scuffing up my faces as he rushed inside, only later realizing that he'd tracked chalk all over the floor. And when he discovered what he'd done, would he see those smears as my sadness, would they seem more than mere chalk?

I returned to my nearly empty apartment and surveyed its comforting, spartan denial; then I pulled out the phone and slept.

My dream had changed. My body was no longer weightless, airy. I was plunging through that limitless darkness, the air pressing against my back. I fell for so long I grew accustomed to the resistance of the wind and barely noticed it. But somewhere in my descent I worried about where I was falling to. Perhaps the pressure I felt wasn't the wind. What if it was the ground? Perhaps I had already landed and was lying on my crushed back. In the complete darkness, how could I be sure? I could certainly try to move my outstretched arms, but I didn't want to finally know.

I remained still until I woke and saw the gray dullness of early morning light. I recognized across from me the outline of my bedroom window, recognized my heart's staggering beat like my own fleeing footsteps. I *have* landed, I thought, right where I'll always land, in my own room. I closed my eyes again but I still saw those same boundaries: the familiar walls and ceiling that will always face me, the same windows and door forever resisting my exit. How can I possibly escape my home when it's inside me?

And I'm not the only one who lives here: I'm bursting with

accommodations for my daily, involuntary family reunion. My sisters, shorn of their current angry husbands and crowd of kids, skulk down a hall. My mother manages to find any unassuming corner, where she keeps to herself behind that maddeningly faint twist in her lips, harboring complexities I can't imagine, and I cannot animate her, I cannot make her speak. My father marches out of his room whenever he wants to command attention, trotting out his repertoire of contempt. "So, you finally inflicted yourself on someone's home," he begins, but I don't have to listen further because I know those terrible words in advance—they're my own, I have them memorized. He's really me, my own harsh and unrelenting critic that I've given my father's face and voice. These phantoms aren't my family—they're familiar faces I've put on my perplexing, hidden impulses.

So I've decided to lie here and design myself a new life, with the freedom of one of those desert nomads who sews the skins of her goat herd to make the family tent. I can feel the thick thread, rough against my dark hands in the dry air, while my children play around me. And I imagine that when my husband and I make our night noises, our thrashing is echoed above by those taut skins skitting in the wind: with my eyes closed and swishing my hands against the bedsheet, I can believe I'm almost there. But first I have to evict my current occupants and empty the rooms, and I'm going to start with Frederick.

He should be the easiest to banish, having spent so short a time here, yet when I try to change his name, his height, his weight and face into someone less Frederick, I never succeed. I can't help returning to the room he occupies inside me. It's empty, with nothing on the walls, not even a window. On the floor is a box of colored chalks I've placed there to force him to imagine his room and sketch a chair against a wall, a sofa in the corner, even draw his own window and fill it in: maybe a city street with a luncheonette and gallery across the street, or a clutch of forest with a path leading into the shadows. But he draws nothing and, as always, he will not speak to me.

Though lately I've noticed Frederick fingering the chalks, and I'm certain that one day he will finally animate his room. When I come to visit there will be a bed drawn on the floor, and a smudgy figure within it left by his body where he slept. On the wall is a shelf, and on the shelf a photograph, though I will not be able to make out the details of the faces. There will also be a window, and a view: a star-filled evening sky, with the dim shadows of mountains on the horizon. His window will look so real he must have tried to force his way through it, because there will be chalk stains on his forehead almost indistinguishable from bruises. I will think that perhaps I misjudged him, perhaps he *had* thought of striking the chair and splintering it in rage and only restrained himself in embarrassment before me. Yet these are thoughts that are not good to think. I won't say one word to him, though he will stand there waiting, and when I leave his room he'll listen to my footsteps down the hall until they can't be heard. He'll wait for the silence to settle and then, if I am very lucky, when he opens the door I will let him make his escape.

Beauty Marks

artin sits on the couch and stares at the papers scattered over the coffee table—it still feels strange writing under a roof instead of the sky in an open African courtyard. Barbara has long since gone off to bed, and maybe now he should take out his secret maps of the Isono farms, examine them. Instead he listens to the faint, familiar mysteries he hadn't known he'd missed: little snaps and disembodied groans from the wooden floors, a sudden whir in the refrigerator, a rush of water down the pipes from another apartment.

He picks up one of his pages and reads: "An Isono can't be given a field to farm until marriage, and one can't be married until initiated and ritually scarred." Martin is certain it's too soon to make sense of this, even if his dissertation advisor *did* say to charge right in. The loops and curves of his handwriting might as well be abstract designs.

In the kitchen the dirty dishes in the sink lose some precarious balance and settle with a quick clatter. My job, Martin thinks, and he walks in and starts washing the evidence of Barbara's attempt at an African dinner. She'd even set a candle on the floor, its flicker evoking village firelight. The okra sauce had really hit the spot, but those balls of Bisquick were poor substitutes for white yams. Still, he'd eaten what he could without complaining, even though each bite made him think of Kwamla, lying wasted on that straw pallet in the village and waving away whatever food his wife, Yani, offered.

Sighing, Martin sets the last dish in the drainer. Outside, an occasional car passes with a soft growl through the sprawling university town. He's restless in these cramped rooms, and hungry. There's an all-night convenience store nearby, so he steps out the door and down the stairs.

Summer is really ending—instead of his body's sticky sweat he feels the unfamiliar rise of goosebumps. Enjoying the strange sensation, he steps quickly down the street, though soon he wishes he'd gone back for a jacket—rain is on the way, and the bare branches above him twist in the cold wind. A few homeless people—poor souls!—huddle under flapping newspapers in the dark alcove of a tobacco shop. They stare through him as he hurries by.

He's thoroughly chilled by the time he pushes open the glass door, the bell chiming behind him, and he walks down fluorescent-lit aisles, past dog food and canned ravioli, past chips of all persuasions. Stopping at the percussive purr of the coffee machine, he pours himself a cup, then slips a plastic-wrapped burger and a pouch of fries in the microwave—anything warm will do.

The oven beeps and he pulls the irradiated things out. Martin forces himself to eat the tough meat, the tasteless dry fries, and he scans the racks of tabloids. Gossip about the dead seems to be a theme this week: Elvis has married Natalie Wood, Ari and Jack have been fighting over Jackie since her arrival, Janis Joplin begs John to forget Yoko. Okay, Martin thinks, so what's an anthropologist to make of all this? The afterlife must be an unexpected hothouse: no rest for the dead, eternal job security for sleazy reporters.

Outside it's drizzling and even colder than before. Martin heads for home in a half-trot. Cars pass by on the wet pavement with a hissing glide, and he begins to run, hoping no patrol car will drive by to see a young man dashing away from a convenience store at night.

Back at the apartment the radiator squeals and grunts as if alive. Martin gently spreads an extra wool blanket over Barbara and slips into bed. She turns in her sleep, and Martin drapes an arm over her waist before drifting into a strange mixture of sleepy images: Kwamla, his face still round and healthy, sits in his mud house before a television, its screen hissing and crackling from bad reception. Martin is beside him, turning the dial for a clear channel, when a phone rings—the distant sound must come from the forest. Kwamla turns his worried face to Martin. "I'll be right back," Martin promises. He runs to the edge of the thick brush and pushes his way through, because it's somehow very important that he find that phone before the ringing stops.

Barbara stirs against Martin, her legs snug against his, and she opens her eyes to a ceiling of white plaster, not thatch. Outside there's the whoosh of morning traffic instead of the pounding of wooden mortars and pestles. She breathes in the dry, heated air, closes her eyes again, and catches the last bit of her dream: Yani's dark face leaning so close and whispering a secret, though Barbara can't hear her, and as Yani's face fades Barbara wishes it had been Martin's—she still hasn't met him in any of her dreams since their return.

She pushes away the blankets. Martin moans sleepily and turns to her, his hair flattened against his head, eyes half open. He smiles and tickles the rise of her ribs.

"How late did you stay up?" she asks.

"Not too late. I jotted down some notes until I almost fell asleep in the chair." His hand slinks up slowly to her breasts.

"What did you dream?"

Martin closes his eyes, appears to concentrate. "I can't remember." He puts his fingers to his lips and whispers, "Hush." Then he's above her, his face looming over hers, and Barbara imagines she's still asleep and dreaming his gentle motions.

For breakfast Martin serves an array of cereal, bacon, buttery waffles, more than she can eat. Watching him gobble down his eggs, Barbara marvels at how easily he's become an American again. She'd prefer sweetened corn porridge but keeps this to herself, knowing that last night's dinner wasn't a success. Maybe this morning would be a good time to write about Isono food taboos.

But at her cluttered desk she can barely concentrate on her list of culinary dos and don'ts—a pregnant woman cannot eat forest snails, palm nut sauce must be prepared on rest days. She stares at the blank computer screen—how is she ever going to translate the complexities of the last year and a half into chapters, footnotes, and references?

Behind her, as if roaming the winding mud alleyways of the village, Martin takes yet another distracting tour of their small apartment. He returns and writes a sentence or two, then wanders the rooms again. Finally he says, "I'm going out for a minute. We're out of coffee."

Barbara looks out the window at Martin walking down the sidewalk and imagines him setting off for the farming fields, leaving her alone again in the village. She and Martin had thought they were so clever, dividing the Isono between them; but as an outsider Martin—to his great frustration—wasn't allowed to enter the fields, and during the planting season there was almost no one left in the village during the day for Barbara to speak to. She often wandered among the compounds, but those irregular networks of mud houses and courtyards were eerily empty: no women pounding yams, no men lazing in the shade gulping palm wine, no shifting groups of playful children.

She was so happy when she finally met Yani. With a newborn, Yani could rest in the village and take care of her infant for months. Wait, Barbara thinks—she turns from the computer

screen and pages through a notebook until she finds that first con-
versation and remembers sitting in Yani's compound. The dark
plaits of Yani's hair had glistened in the sun, and she bent her soft
face over her daughter Amwe while Barbara administered drops
in the red, crusty eyes of the whimpering infant. Yani sang a few
lines of a song in a sweet, high-pitched voice, and Barbara asked
Yani what the song was about, a question she had to repeat in her
imperfect Isono.

Yani lifted her eyes and said, "Do you see the clear sky? It's a
song to ward off drought." She spoke slowly, so Barbara could
translate and write the words down:

> *The smooth stones of the empty river bed*
> *Are the flat bellies of our hungry children*
> *May it rain, rain and never stop!*

Yani looked with amusement at the frantic movement of Barbara's hand, then cradled her suddenly restless, wailing baby, and
Barbara ventured to make her first joke in Isono: "Maybe that's
not Amwe's favorite song."

"No," Yani murmured, loosening her cloth wrapper. She fit a
breast to her baby's wide mouth. "She's crying over some mistake she made in her last life."

"*Last* life?" Barbara said, thinking she misunderstood.

"Yes, all babies can remember their past lives," Yani replied,
again speaking slowly enough for Barbara to follow. "When they
cry, they're remembering a sadness; when they laugh, an old happiness." She looked down at her quietly nursing daughter.
"When they're silent, no one knows what they're thinking."

"Could she tell you when she grows up?" Barbara asked, scribbling more notes, delighted with this talkative young woman.

Yani swatted a fly away from her baby's face and continued.
"When babies finally speak their first word, they make their
choice for this life. They forget the past."

"But how do you know they forget?"

Yani paused, seemingly entranced at the depths of ignorance revealed by Barbara's question, and then she said, "If I could remember my past life, I wouldn't have made the mistakes I've made in this one. If my eyes are open, why should I stumble?"

Now Barbara turns back to the blank screen. Why indeed? she thinks, and types, "The Isono's chain of lives is divided by an unbridgeable gap of memory." Barbara pauses, wonders what her friend might make of this sentence, and as she continues to write she worries whether she's moving closer to or farther away from the Isono.

Martin chews his pen and stares at the latest version of his latest sentence: "The Isono practice an agricultural expressionism at odds with their usual social constraints." Where should he go from here? Barbara's swift clacking at the computer behind him sounds like the collective scraping of hand hoes against the ground, and when he closes his eyes he could still be sitting at the edge of those clearings in the forest, unable to enter, watching lines of men and women scraping and piling soil into small pyramids where yams would soon grow.

Occasionally Martin had touched a sandaled toe to a tiny corn stalk for a secret thrill when no one was looking. Why couldn't that have been enough for him—when he did manage to sneak into those fields, what good had it done him?

If only someone had answered his questions! "Why plant corn here, yams over there?" he once called out to Busu, a frail-looking elder who somehow worked harder than anyone else. But the old man merely said, "You would only understand if you were an Isono," adding with a wry smile, "and then there would be no need to speak."

Martin tried Kwamla, hoping he would be as talkative as his wife, Yani. "Why do you arrange your fields differently from Goli and Aia?" he asked. Kwamla averted his eyes, staring down at the soil, and said, "That's our custom."

At Martin's exasperated frown Kwamla grinned and put down

his hoe. The elaborate scarification marks on his stomach were dark sweaty beads, and he looked so healthy then. He mimicked holding a notebook and wagged a finger across an invisible page. "Why do you always make marks on paper?"

Martin laughs quietly now, as he did then. He picks up his pen, murmurs, "It's our custom," and tries another sentence: "The crop organization of the farming fields is an unusual form of individual expression in a society of such tight social constraints." But wait, he thinks, didn't I just write something like that?

He looks over to Barbara. Her head is bent toward the computer, all those little green words shining back at her on the dark screen—how easy it is for her to write.

"Barb, I'm going to stretch my legs outside for a bit."

She barely nods, keeps clacking away.

He wears a jacket this time, zipped up tight before he hits the sidewalk. Intent on walking nowhere in particular, Martin continues block after block, past clusters of shops and apartments. Down a side street, he stops: near the back of a restaurant an old man in a frayed, dark coat is poking through a dumpster, dropping who knows what into a plastic garbage bag. What will happen to him when it's really cold—isn't there a shelter to go to?

Martin backs up, turns down another street, and sees a shining movie marquee. He realizes with some surprise that he and Barbara still haven't been to a movie since their return. But no one's in the ticket booth, and he can see through the glass door that the concession stand is deserted, too. The last show must be ending and the employees are puttering around in the office. He slips inside and can just make out muffled car squeals and gun shots, a pulsating soundtrack. Why not take a quick peek? He hurries through the empty lobby, glancing back and forth nervously.

"Hey, you!" someone shouts behind him. Martin pushes through swinging doors into the darkened theater and a spectacular, technicolor car crash. Half stumbling down the aisle, he ducks into the first empty seat.

As his eyes adjust to the darkness he watches an usher pace

halfheartedly with a flashlight. The minimum wage certainly isn't worth any possible trouble from finding me, Martin thinks, and anyway, for all he knows I'm just a homeless guy looking for a little warmth. All around him faces are turned up to the giant screen. Martin can't imagine what an Isono villager might make of the swift pace of images: cars give chase, cars collide, cars overturn. Martin eases into his chair and breathes in the salty essence of popcorn.

Still awake in bed, Barbara listens to the click of the front door, then Martin's footsteps to the edge of the bed—he's back from wherever. She's insulted that he assumes she's asleep: it would be nice if he said Hello, or at least whisper Good Night. But when he lies down beside her his palm cups a shoulder blade, squeezes. His fingers slip along the smooth bumps down the ridge of her spine, and this reminds her of the Isono scarification marks: those little raised knobs of flesh forming unpredictable swirling patterns, interwoven arcs and circles. Martin traces patterns against the tight muscles of her back and she stirs, slowly pressing her ankle up the length of his leg.

In the morning Barbara pages through her folder of the Isono scarification designs, laughing when she thinks that at first she and Martin called them beauty marks, a kind of jewelry that lasted a lifetime. How lucky she'd been one morning, when during her route of greetings she came upon a tense village meeting. The elders sat upright in a semicircle of wooden stools, wearing colored robes slung over the shoulder, facing two young men she had never seen before, dressed in sleek, well-tailored shirts and pants.

Something secret was up, because just as one of the young men began speaking rapidly to the elders—the cigarette dangling from his mouth obviously an act of bravado—an old woman came up to Barbara and offered to show her a stash of traditional cloth. To refuse an invitation was extremely impolite, so Barbara pretended she misheard. "Tomorrow? Yes, I'll come, then. Many thanks," she said. But before she could ease away, a thin, firm hand was on her shoulder: the old woman spoke slowly and clearly, determined to be understood.

When Yani came by later that day for more medicine—her frail daughter was ill again—she sat down by the desk under the palm frond veranda and anxiously watched Barbara spread cream over Amwe's rash. "I'm afraid that my cousin is bewitching my child. Her own child was born breech and died—she's surely jealous . . ."

Yani recounted her fears while Barbara made careful notes on what types of relatives could bewitch each other. Yet when Yani was done, Barbara couldn't help asking, "Who were those two men at the trial this morning?"

Yani was silent. She cradled her child and stared off at the huge wall of trees surrounding the village, until finally Barbara said, "Yani, we're friends. How can I truly understand you if I don't understand your people?"

Yani stood up. "I don't think I can talk with you any more," she said sadly. "Our farm isn't strong this season, and I need to work in the fields more."

It was true that the sporadic rains might not produce the best harvest, but Barbara would not let herself lose Yani. She took a handful of bills from her pocket, blushing at her own bravado. "This won't make the rains come, but it can help pay for medicines and divinations for your daughter's illness. Take these," she pleaded. "In my country, words are valuable."

Yani hesitated, glancing about her, and then, with perhaps an admiring smile at Barbara's argument, took the money and slipped it under the waistband of her skirt. She sat back down on her stool.

"Who were those men?" Barbara asked again, but still Yani sat mute, though now she fixed her eyes carefully on the battered manual typewriter on the desk. Barbara understood: the Isono considered the clatter of typing ugly—the noise kept most villagers from the courtyard. She slipped a piece of paper in the typewriter and began pounding away Yani's name, the date, and the question she had just asked, and then she tapped comma after comma across the page while she waited.

Yani flinched at the sound, but it was her protection. "They were born in this village, and their families worked hard to send them to the university." Yani spat, one of those marvelous arcs the villagers were so good at. "Now, because they live in the city and work in a government office, they think they aren't Isono."

Barbara typed this out and asked, "Why do you say that?"

Yani looked away, tucked her baby closer to her breast. "They have told the elders they won't allow themselves to be scarred in this year's ritual."

"Oh. But why is that so terrible?"

Yani hesitated. Marking time, Barbara banged away plus and minus signs until Yani said, "They won't be able to marry an Isono girl."

"Why?"

"Because they will never become Isono."

"Really? What *will* they become?"

"They will become no one."

"Why?" Barbara asked again. She pressed the space bar until the bell pinged and Yani finally said, "Every Isono has a spirit living within." Avoiding Barbara's startled gaze, Yani looked away. Then she said, so slowly, so quietly, "When I feel an itch, it's the spirit rubbing against me inside. Our scarification designs reveal our spirits' paths."

Exhilarated, Barbara typed out Yani's answer and then a barrage of exclamation points. Listening to the happy squeals of children running down the convoluted alleyways of a nearby compound, she wanted to join them, hooting with pleasure.

Instead she asked, "But why are the designs only on the stomach?"

"A spirit travels everywhere in the body, but its true home is here," Yani said, gesturing from her chest to her waist. "It wants to be born, just as a baby kicks in the womb."

Again Barbara clattered away, asking, "What happens during the ritual?"

"The diviner sees, from the points that itch, the hidden design. But why ask any more questions? You can see the women's initiation tomorrow."

Now Barbara regards the pages of this interview: a typed crazy quilt of oddly spaced questions and answers and repeated punctuation marks of all assortments. How different this looks from her sparse notes on the ritual.

She had stood among the silent crowd and watched the young girls of the village lying on their backs, eyes tightly closed, waiting. The diviner was Mokla—the same old woman who had led Barbara away from the trial—and she was dressed in white, kneeling before an animal skin and arranging a knife, small chunks of charcoal, a pile of ash. When she noticed Barbara she scowled. Barbara set her notebook and pen down on the ground and stepped back a few paces, until Mokla turned away from her.

Then the diviner moved among the initiates, murmuring words Barbara couldn't make out. Slowly, the girls began pointing with trembling hands to this itching spot, that one, and Mokla marked the points with a piece of charcoal. When those asymmetrical, elegant patterns were done, Mokla pinched the first girl's skin between thumb and forefinger, slit it, and applied ash to make the wound pucker and darken. None of the girls screamed despite the pain on their faces, the blood dribbling down their sides, and soon Mokla's white gown was stained with red streaks. Without her notebook Barbara had to watch carefully, but it was hard, so hard.

After the ritual, Barbara stayed in their hut for days, dizzy at the thought of that bloodletting. Martin sweetly stayed with her and claimed she had malaria, thanking all the villagers who wished her good health. But she knew her husband was anxious to return to the fields. He wanted to puzzle out a recent mystery: even though the corn crop had suddenly become infested with caterpillars, the elders declared that no one could kill them.

Finally one morning Martin said, "The Isono may not have a word for privacy, but I'll bet before long they'll have one because of us."

Ashamed of her weakness, she told herself the ritual wasn't mutilation—no, not at all—it was art. In a culture where the women improvised patterns on manioc cakes before baking them, and even children sliced designs into orange rinds, the diviners were the supreme artists. When Barbara finally left the hut, determined to overcome her squeamishness, she began to ask villagers if she could draw their scarred designs.

Now Barbara leans back from the computer and peers out the window, hoping to see Martin. He's left her alone again, off on another errand. Why don't *I* go out? she wonders—It's not as if I'm confined to an Isono compound. Sighing, she rests her hands on the keys, then types, "The scars are maps of the interior: the body is a spirit's abode, and a spirit is a guest each Isono must accommodate." She glances down at her drawing of one of the designs, can almost see blood flow out from the scarred points.

Martin sets the bags of groceries down on the counter. Barbara's sketches of Isono body decorations are everywhere, littering the walls, the refrigerator, the kitchen cabinets—they're even taped up on the backs of the chairs. I suppose I deserve this, he thinks. Pulling cheese and packaged tomatoes from a bag, he wishes that he had the luxury of using his maps of the Isono farm plots. But how could he ever explain to Barbara why he's kept them from her?

She walks in and without a word helps carry bottles of juice to the refrigerator. Martin approaches one of her sketches threateningly. "Where's my pen?" he asks. "I have a sudden urge to play connect-the-dots."

"C'mon, stop. They're for inspiration," she says.

"Oh really? Are you thinking about starting up an Isono beauty parlor?" And now he just can't help himself, he searches through a drawer and says, "Let me get the knife sharpener. . . ."

Barbara slams shut the refrigerator and leaves the room.

"Hey, only kidding," he says, shaken, his voice small.

Frustrated that he can't use what he's not supposed to know, Martin pushes pork cutlets into the oven, chops away at vegetables, and then stirs and stirs them in a pan. If only he hadn't lingered behind at the end of that workday, at the edge of the already damaged fields. Because of the sparse rain the corn was barely waist high, the yam vines were just beginning to poke up from the dirt mounds, and everywhere were signs of the caterpillars' hunger. Martin watched one of those voracious creatures efficiently chew a path through a corn leaf. Fascinated, he drew closer, and the caterpillar, at the end of the leaf, reared up briefly. Along its pale underbelly were dark, convoluted patterns, and then Martin knew why no Isono would dare touch one.

"You're lucky you were born with those beauty marks, huh," he whispered. He took out his notebook, listened to the distant cries of a flock of birds, the flutter of corn leaves in the wind— no, it sounded like something was creeping through the stalks. Martin crouched down: maybe this was some foraging animal he should warn the Isono about. He peered in.

Kwamla, hunched down, was crawling along with a sharpened stick. He flicked a caterpillar from a corn leaf and then impaled it against the ground. When he turned to slip the crushed insect into a cloth bag he saw Martin.

Kwamla sat up, the broad green leaves waving in the wind around his shoulders, his face filled with something like terror. "No one must know," he said, "no one must know."

Martin almost whispered back, "No one will," but instead he waited, curious how Kwamla would react to his silence.

A few long moments passed, and then quietly, with a resigned gesture of his hand, Kwamla said, "Come." He motioned to his fields, to those private, winding paths, and Martin understood this was a gift for his silence.

Martin hesitated, accepted. He took out his notebook and, carefully counting the number of steps he took along each little trail, quickly roughed out the arrangement of crops. But he needed two, maybe three more maps for a decent comparative study. So when he finished his map he stared off at Goli's neighboring farm, turned to Kwamla and said, "No one will know." Kwamla winced at this echo of his words, then took a few steps into Goli's field, and Martin followed, his shame rising.

"What's that burning?" Barbara shouts from the living room. Martin looks down—the vegetables are scorched in the pan. He hurries the mess over to the sink, leaving a trail of smoke behind him.

They eat what's left of dinner in silence—Barbara must still be annoyed at him for his nasty little joke. By way of apology, knowing she hasn't been out of the apartment for days, he asks, "Hey, you want to catch a movie tonight?"

"No," she says, barely looking up, "I have to work. I'm in the middle of something right now." And you're not, he imagines her thinking.

While she washes the dishes he slips out for another of his nightly tours. He walks faster now through the cold air, ranging from street to street, but when he skirts a small lot he stops, surprised to see two bundled figures—a man, a woman—crouching against a fence, beside a shopping cart stuffed with clothes. Why aren't they at the shelter? He imagines a large room, rows and rows of cots: maybe it's not quite cold enough to venture to the common misery, the lack of privacy.

Martin would like to talk to them, even offer some help, but he's also afraid somehow, and he marches off in another direction. Curious to see if he can actually become lost, he wanders down one street after another, through neighborhoods he's never seen, until he approaches a busy bar, a line of motorcycles parked beneath the neon signs advertising different brands of beer. A rough crowd lounges by the door: leather jackets with sewn patches of skulls, sharks, lightning. Interesting iconography, Martin thinks, but such a limited repertoire of acceptable images. He slowly passes by a man with long dark hair framing a pockmarked face: on his leather jacket are pictures of two bloody fists, and there's a tattoo on one of his wrists—the end of a snake's tail, perhaps, or a dragon's.

The man grins at him. "Hey, you staring at me?"

Martin tries to smile back. "No, not at all."

"The hell you're not." He flicks out a knife.

Martin runs away from the sudden laughter behind him and turns swiftly down one side street, then another. But he's not sure if the steps he hears are merely the echo of his own. Looking back, Martin sees nothing, but it's dark—Who can tell, he thinks, who can tell? He stops short and crouches beside a mailbox, waiting for the sound of pursuing footsteps.

Barbara listens to Martin close the door behind him, his faint steps down the stairs—every night now he goes out, sometimes for hours. Why won't he tell her where he's off to, why can't she simply ask him? Maybe she should follow along, take a break and not work so hard. But Barbara hesitates, remembering ruefully the Isono's two phrases for marriage that Yani taught her: the men's phrase, "To offer a road," and the women's, "To follow behind."

Yani's soft face had been pinched that day with anxiety over Kwamla. "What can I do?" she said. "He eats almost nothing, he refuses to see a diviner. I know he's being bewitched, because our farm has done so well while others have done so poorly."

Barbara murmured sympathy—the poor man looked so thin and haunted. Suddenly there arose in a nearby compound the usual angry hubbub of Yao and Sunu, a newly married couple.

Yani clicked her tongue, continued nursing Amwe. "Those two—their scars don't match. The paths of their spirits rarely touch." Barbara slipped a piece of paper into the typewriter and tapped away while Yani said, "In the best marriages the scarification designs become full during lovemaking, when the scars rub and fit together." As if ashamed of her words, Yani stopped.

"But you," she said suddenly, staring hard at Barbara's face, "how can you know your husband if you don't know the movements of his spirit?"

"Good question," Barbara says now to the empty room. She rubs her back against the chair, imagining an Isono couple making love with those curving ridges of skin: their dark bodies elaborate mazes leading to each other, nipples rubbing against chest scars, fingers following the raised marks, the patterns channels for sweat.

Barbara pushes away from the computer and stands up: after burrowing for so long into their culture, now the Isono are burrowing into her. Her back itches, just beneath her left shoulder blade where she can't reach. She grabs a pen, bends her arm back awkwardly, and rubs until the tingling is satisfied.

There's a slight tickle just below her ribs, and before she scratches that too she imagines a design of ridges tingling her entire body—smooth, hairless nobs of skin hidden beneath her clothes. Why not turn the pen's felt tip around and mark the itch? Barbara laughs nervously, but she pulls up her blouse and draws a nice, dark dot. Another itch rises up, just below her left breast, and she marks that spot with a deft touch of the pen. Then she strips off her blouse and bra and continues a careful catalogue of sudden itches that seem to have no relation to thought or intention.

Barbara stares down at her torso, foolishly inked all over. Beauty marks indeed. The points scattered below her breasts and the wavering line leading across her stomach aren't beautiful at all—merely signs of a lopsided and aimless spirit. What if we returned to the Isono with our bodies speckled with pen marks? We could tell them that in our country initiations are performed after marriage, that we only *draw* our spirits' travels and then chart new paths once the old ones wear off. But Barbara imagines an elder asking, "Why do your spirits change their paths so often—why are they so restless?"

The radiator begins to clank—it's cold outside, and Martin could come home any moment. What would he say if he saw her like this? She pads to the bathroom and takes a shower. Dark inky stains slip down her body like bloody trails, and Barbara shudders. She scrubs and scrubs until it hurts.

Martin makes himself sit at his damned desk and tries to rework another sentence: "Isono farms are exclusionary space that admit no strangers. Here, apparently, is where one truly becomes Isono." He puts down the pen. Kwamla would have felt guilty whether I found him killing those bugs or not, Martin tells himself, and I did keep my promise—I didn't tell anyone, not even my wife. What more could I have done? On his last day in the village Martin spent hours at Kwamla's compound. Sitting beside his friend and trying not to stare at his wasted body, Martin waited for a brief moment when they would be alone. "Please don't die, please," he'd finally whispered. "I'll never tell anyone." Stretched out on a palm frond chair, Kwamla merely offered a wan smile, his thin face a mask Martin couldn't read.

He stirs his coffee until it's tepid. Behind him, Barbara clatters away at the computer—all day she's been stuck to the chair. Martin sighs and puts on his heavy coat, though he doesn't want to go out, afraid of where he'll find himself this time. He walks to the door, sure that Barbara is watching him.

"Where are you going?"

His hand grips the doorknob but he doesn't turn around. "Nowhere in particular—just a walk."

He hears her press the Save button. The computer's contented grunting starts up.

"Please don't go."

"I'll be back soon."

"Please don't go."

Though Martin doesn't reply, he doesn't move either. "Do you want to come along?"

"Why don't you stay and work?"

He turns and strides toward her, anger rising up from who

knows where. "Just what makes you think I'm *not* working when I walk?"

Barbara hesitates. "Your desk. When you're gone I don't see any writing being done."

"It's in *here*," he says, pointing at his head.

"Oh, very good." Barbara mimicks his gesture and taps at her forehead. "Is this what you'll do at your thesis defense? Think you'll pass?"

"Shut up. Worry about *yourself*. Keep pecking, pecking, *pecking* away!" His rage is a thing that must be shaken loose, and he sweeps stacks of papers from his desk. They scatter on the floor and Martin, so embarrassed, wants to escape the apartment even more. He slams the door behind him.

It's so cold outside—he can't take these walks much longer, and he paces himself as if trying to hurry away from his unfairness to Barbara, breath fanning out and dissipating before him as he huffs down avenues and short alleys. No homeless people out tonight, thank God.

Passing through a neighborhood of single-story boxes he hears the distant blare of a bell, an alarm, perhaps. Martin crosses a main road and follows the noise down a long stretch of small stores to a hat shop at the end of the block. It *is* an alarm—someone tried to break in.

The window display is bathed in a gray sheen from the street lamps. Martin draws closer, looks inside. The dim light in the back of the store casts odd shadows, and those clusters of hat racks could be a forest found nowhere else: stunted trees weighted with strange, bulbous fruit. Watching his reflection in the window, Martin moves as if he's actually skulking in there—he raises an arm and his shadowy fingers try to pluck a fruit from a branch. He stops. There he is—the thief in the field. He leans closer, presses his hand against its image, feels the plate glass vibrating from the alarm.

A police car roars down the avenue, its light flashing. For a moment Martin stands there before the store as if exposed, caught, and then he dashes off, the siren wailing behind him. What am I *doing* to myself? he thinks, but he doesn't slow down, racing into the shadows of a side street, then cutting across a dark yard.

He crouches behind the shrubs along a darkened house and waits. Through the branches, eerie streaks of light and dark are cast by the police car's cherry top as it passes. Then the lights go on in the window above him and Martin tears off, crossing an empty street. Another police car passes by the intersection and stops. He rushes away from its siren, across another backyard. Hopping a fence, he hurtles through the dark, down a line of trees—a sort of alley between backyards. I'm only guilty if I'm caught, he thinks, stray branches scratching his face. I have to get back home, back home. His chest aching from the cold, Martin stops at the thought of facing Barbara: how much longer can he keep his secret from her? I should just rip up those maps, just rip them up!

Then Martin continues to run down that alley of trees until he comes to the dead end of a brick garage. Somewhere behind him a dog growls and barks. Kneeling in the dark, he grabs a smooth, oval stone, vaguely remembers an Isono song Barbara once mentioned to him—something about a drought—and waits for the sound of swift, padding feet. But when he hears the dog straining against a chain fence he cuts through a garden, a playground, and then an unlit parking lot.

The sirens now seem closer, and Martin stops at the edge of the street, at first afraid to cross the open space. At the other side is a blanketed figure, curled up on the sidewalk over a library's heating grate. The perfect place to hide, Martin thinks, sprinting across the street. He lies down on the steel grid and slips under an edge of the blanket.

He smells stale breath and looks at the sleeping man beside him: his mouth is half open, a dark space where his front teeth should be. Trying not to move, Martin rests his face against the steel grid of the grate and feels the welcome heat rising up, his face tingling as he lies still, minute after minute slowly passing.

The interlocking sirens suddenly sound louder, and the man beside him stirs and turns. Martin can see traces of the grate's pattern marked on the man's stubbly cheek: little squares echoing along the jaw line. Martin traces his fingers against the slight imprints on his own cheek, tries to imagine the design—his own beauty marks. Well, well, he thinks, this has been one hell of an initiation.

A siren wails nearby and the man stirs again, his brow crinkled from troubles Martin can't imagine: on a night like this he must have nowhere to go. Or perhaps this grate is his last, tiny spot of territory. Ah, *trespassing* again. Suddenly, desperately, he needs to confess to someone, anyone, he needs this stranger's forgiveness. And if I *do* confess, Martin thinks, if he'd even listen to my story, would he let me stay here and hide? Martin has to know. The man smacks his cracked lips in half-sleep—he might wake at any moment—and Martin reaches out under the blanket, certain that a gentle nudge is all that's needed.

Barbara stares mournfully at Martin's pages scattered at her feet and wishes she hadn't been so cruel. But did he have to leave? She's so afraid she'll mark herself up again while he's gone. Barbara bends down, about to busy herself with picking up the batches of pages, when she notices rough diagrams of some sort: she reads measurements, the names of crops.

They're maps of the Isono farms. Somehow Martin managed to sneak in and draw these . . . and he hid them, she realizes, he *hid* them! Yet Barbara manages to check her anger—one of the maps lying next to her looks oddly familiar, even if it's upside-down. She flips it around and glances at Martin's angular scrawl in the corner, identifying Yani and Kwamla's farm. Strange—now it doesn't look familiar. Turning the page upside-down again, Barbara leans over, peers closely until it seems her hands can feel the individual nubs of the carpet, and she shivers: it's as if Yani is before her.

Barbara scrambles to the desk, searches through a folder for her own sketches, finds Yani's scarifications, and compares them with the farm: they're almost certainly the same design! She sits down, nearly breathless, and then, wondering if this pattern repeats itself elsewhere, she jumps up and quickly pages through one of her notebooks. She'd once mapped out Yani's compound—would that match too?

Her crude map doesn't look anything like the other two, no matter which way she turns it. But there's more, she knows there *must* be more. She pulls out her picture of Kwamla's scarifications and places it beside the compound. Again, no match. But on a hunch Barbara turns the compound sketch upside-down: the asymmetrical arrangement of courtyards and mud huts, the clusters of beaded scars, are virtually identical.

Feeling as if secret paths are being cleared inside her, Barbara recalls the ritual for a new compound, when the entire village would walk through it, following the head of the household and his wife. And then the Isono, so far away, rear up to engulf Barbara and her faltering understanding: to walk down those convoluted alleyways, she thinks, must be like a spirit tracing the same paths inside the body. The Isono were making familiar landscapes for their spirits!

But upside-down? She arranges the designs on the coffee table and stares and stares. Nothing comes to her, but her own strange tracery of paths within makes Barbara willing to attempt anything now, and she picks up her sketch of Yani's scars and places it against her own stomach. Trying to imagine Yani planning the arrangement of crops, she looks down, and there is the design of the farm. *Of course*—hadn't Yani said that a spirit wishes to be born? So its paths should face down, like an infant in the womb. From an Isono's perspective, this must be the true way to view the scars. Barbara walks back and forth across the room, anxious, shamed. My god, I drew all the designs *upside-down*. Why didn't anyone tell me?

Because we were outsiders, strangers, she realizes with a rush of sadness. But now I know, *now* I know! Barbara flips on the computer and types every interpretation she can think of until her fingers begin to tingle, until she's even sure she understands why outsiders aren't allowed to enter the fields: the farms must be a kind of sacred space, where the spirits are reborn each year when the crops rise.

The sudden wail of distant police sirens breaks Barbara's concentration, and she stops and scans row after electronic row. She's come up with speculation, nothing more. The wall of bright green words facing her on the dark screen looks like the forest that surrounded and locked the village into its own curious energies, but now suddenly lit up and phosphorescent in the night. Even the howling of those sirens outside sounds like some nocturnal forest animal.

If only I'd known enough to ask the right questions, she thinks, would Yani have shared these secrets with someone who wasn't Isono, or had our intimacy really been false, a joke? Imagining Yani in the room with her, just out of sight, Barbara asks, "Were we friends?" There's no answer.

And what about Martin's betrayal? They were supposed to share *all* their data. How could he have possibly kept these maps from her, how can he leave her alone night after night in this apartment? He's as much a stranger as Yani, Barbara thinks, yet he's not here to answer questions either—who knows where he is or when he'll return. She stares at the screen, as if those words might help her understand the mystery of her husband. She sighs, turns off the computer.

Her eyes hurt. It's time to sleep. Slowly Barbara prepares for bed. Again and again, as she brushes her teeth, washes her tired face and then undresses, she pauses, thinking she hears a key turning in the door.

But even when she's lying in the dark under the thick covers Martin still hasn't returned. And then, as though she hasn't wearily closed her eyes, Barbara is back in an Isono compound, but she's not sure which one. The sky is black, moonless: on such a night, with just a few steps the village could suddenly become a dark maze. She's lost.

Or perhaps Martin is lost and she's searching for him. Barbara feels her way forward cautiously in the dark by touching the rough edges of the cool mud walls. A piece breaks off, but she can't hear it fall. Barbara listens to the strange silence—no baby's wail or distant laughter, no insistent insect hum from the forest. She hears Martin now—a sharp cough, almost like a door clicking open. She's certain he's looking for her too—there are his footsteps—but where are the compound's corridors leading him? Barbara feels her way forward slowly, hoping that Martin is doing the same. At any moment he could be just around the next turn. And then, through the darkness, there's his hand on her shoulder, gently shaking her as if she's been asleep.

The Pose

In Isabel's dream a baby floats inside her, in cushiony water that amplifies her heartbeat and stomach gurglings, even the far-away murmur of her already familiar voice. Her baby is a curled inner ear, but against such enveloping noise it folds slowly into its own silence, into a tiny, tightening knot. When Isabel feels a sharp cramp she knows what is shrinking within her. Desperate to draw her baby back from its vanishing, she coos, then cries, then screams out words of endearment until she awakes, still childless.

Morning light slants through the blinds. Isabel hurries from the bed and her still-sleeping husband, as if she could escape this recurring dream that mimics her miscarriages, escape what it releases inside her. One morning just last week she wanted so badly to slam the windows of the house up and down and shatter each pane. Now Isabel stands near the top of the stairs and regards the throw rug at her feet, with its diagonal pattern of white Vs over a blue weave that seems like a flight of birds. Nudging a slipper under the rug's tangled fringe, she's tempted to kick it in the air and watch it try to fly before it tumbles down.

She resists the impulse and steps lightly over the rug, but a faint tick on the third stair down sounds like an infant's hiccup and her feet are suddenly fluid, not her own. She bounds down the stairs to the kitchen, where she stops and stares at the white refrigerator door. How easy it would be to reach in, turn off the thermostat, and wait for everything to warm and spoil. If only she were working her register at Discount Palace, she could suppress these terrible impulses by ringing up lipstick, comic books, pliers, anything—but her next shift is two days away, and she needs to be distracted now. Isabel opens the white door carefully—an elaborate breakfast might be a good way to start the day, something Richard might actually notice when he finally wakes up.

After she slips in the muffin tray and sets the dial, Isabel stares out at the street through the blinds. Soon the young women with their toddlers will stroll by: Doris and her weepy boy, Tammy's girls, Marilyn and the twins—she could name and name them, and all just on this block—and none of them will even glance at her window as they pass.

Upstairs, Richard's morning noises begin—the slide of the closet door, the wooden tug of drawers—and she hurries to lay out the breakfast spread.

Richard enters the kitchen slowly, plucking at his shirt with his good hand—a bit of thread hangs from a loose button.

"Good morning," she whispers.

"Morning, honey," he says to the plate as he sits down, then scratches at the stubble on his chin. Why does he have to stop shaving whenever there's a layoff?

Isabel lifts the pitcher of orange juice. "It's fresh," she says, and Richard raises his glass, eyes tracing idly over the table. She slits open a corn muffin and holds out half. "For you," she says, but he's already dabbing toast into an egg yolk and doesn't hear. His thin mouth moves so slowly he might as well be dreaming breakfast.

There's a good deal she could do to announce herself: sweep

the sugar bowl into his lap, swing cups and saucers into the air. Instead, grasping the edge of the table to keep her arms down, Isabel concentrates on Richard as he spreads his good hand through his hair, tugs at his ear. He picks up the coffee cup, fingers fretting against the warm enamel, and she listens to the dull tap-tap and the slosh of hot coffee inside.

His bad hand rests on the table. Even after a year she's still shocked by the abrupt end of his forefinger, the missing tip of his thumb. Simply lying there, those fleshy stubs seem like knuckles curling inward, his hand about to ball into a fist and smash smash smash. When Isabel starts to think of Richard by a conveyor belt, something mechanical and dark surging toward his careless fingers, she has to look away.

His listless chewing finally over, Richard pushes away from the table, and she knows what he'll say before he says it: "That was good." He retreats to the living room. Left alone, Isabel wants to pour coffee over her still-untouched eggs and drown those two staring eyes.

She hears the porch screen door swing open, then slam shut, and there are Richard's footsteps back to the couch, the newspaper ruffling open, pages turning. She'd prefer him to grumble, even shout about foreign imports and plant closings, this latest layoff. Instead, those scratchy squeaks start: with a magic marker he's unloosing dark lines, blacking out every reference to the Japanese. When he finishes off the yen and Tokyo, Sony, Toyota, and Mitsubishi, she knows that he'll search for soy sauce on the recipe page, bonsai in the gardening section. Then he'll start in on NAFTA and GATT.

Isabel washes each dish slowly until she hears Richard's steps crossing the living room to his workshop, and soon he's hammering away at another one of those projects she can't keep track of, something he hopes will interest an investor.

The dishes done, Isabel ventures to her jigsaw puzzle on the dining room table and peers at the face fit together by bright and convoluted shapes: a wholesome TV actress she can't quite place, perhaps some wisdom-dispensing wife or mom. But there's something unsettling in the anticipation of those eyes, and Isabel wishes she'd picked up a different puzzle at the thrift shop, even one of those impossible abstract paintings.

Only a few pieces remain. The dark grain of the table shines through where the mouth and chin should be. A bittersweet whine of struck metal continues in the workshop, and with a fingernail Isabel traces the hairline cracks that curl about the puzzle face like curiously shaped scars. Then she slips in enough pieces to complete the mouth. The affectionate patience around those lips looks so effortless, and Isabel remembers her own, younger face: Richard had just given her a pair of long white gloves—one of his first gifts—and then he took her picture again and again. She's sure at least one of those snaps lies stacked in a box upstairs.

She spreads the photos before her on the dresser and picks through them carefully. There she is at her high school graduation, wearing a dark robe and standing before a burgundy curtain, her smile fixed with a carefully practiced joy that now seems almost frightening. But this isn't what Isabel is searching for.

Then she finds it: beside a luminous window of afternoon sun, she's settled back in a cushioned chair, legs crossed, mouth half parted, and eyes oval. Her hands look so extraordinarily long and slender in the white gloves. When she had opened the slim box Richard said, "I saw them and they reminded me of your name—crazy, huh?" Those few words—any words, really—were a lot for him, so he hid behind his camera, snapping flash after flash. Isabel remembers she was about to laugh "Enough!" when Richard set his camera on the rug.

Because he approached her with something like awe, she sat still on the chair. Though surprised when he began to slip off the white gloves, she held out her hands and enjoyed the smooth fabric sliding from her fingers. Then he knelt down before her and, after a brief hesitation, just as carefully took off her shoes.

He paused again, and Isabel wondered what this shy man could possibly be doing, until he reached up to unbutton her blouse. She closed her eyes and anticipated his touch against each button. When he slipped the blouse from her shoulders, then unhooked her bra, she rubbed her toes against the nubs of worn wool on the rug and listened to cars passing on the street below—so many and so far away. Only then did she wonder if perhaps she should have whispered *No, no,* or at least tried to squirm away. But his fingers were at her elastic waistband and she lifted herself slightly as he eased off her skirt, her panties.

He knelt before her, his head just touching her knees. For a long silence Isabel could feel the chair's thick weave against her skin, Richard's light breath on her shins. A sudden shout outside and then a burst of wild laughter startled Isabel, and she glanced down at Richard just as he looked up at her. They laughed too, untangling their little knot of quiet, and into that small room the world returned—more cars, footsteps on the pavement, the distant rattle of construction. Richard moved back and gathered together her scattered clothes.

He fit her gloves back on and she finally felt exposed, sitting there naked except for her bright white hands. When Richard approached with her panties she stood up to make it easy for him and his hands rose lightly up her thighs. Then his fingers were against her spine while he fastened her bra, and she wanted him to cup her breasts with his hands but was relieved when he didn't—somehow a caress would have broken this long, strange moment. Finally dressed, her body still buzzing, she giddily considered this a kind of marriage proposal.

If only Isabel could will herself back into the moment of this photograph, but again there's that awful hammering downstairs. She glances at her dresser—those gloves are still in the bottom of some drawer and perhaps she should go look, even allow herself the feel of them again. And what was Richard wearing—wasn't it a white shirt with wide front pockets? Does he still have it? She walks to his closet and slides open the door—it's almost cool inside, and the shadowy row of his clothes draws her in. She pokes through the crisp smells of Richard's shirts until, instead of a shoulder's yielding curve of corduroy or wool, she touches the metal edge of a hanger that jangles oddly.

Isabel pushes aside the shirts. Before her sways a peculiar construction of clothes hangers, elaborately fit together into the full-sized outline of a person. But this flat thing doesn't have a face, only a wire circle for a head, and from its top the hanger hook rises like a question mark. Whatever this is, it isn't finished yet: there's only one wire leg, and even that has no foot. She reaches out and pulls the figure toward her, and it slides awkwardly along the wooden rod, both jointed arms swinging independently. Half expecting resistance, Isabel reaches into its empty chest, then pulls her hand away. How could Richard be making such a thing?

He sets down his hammer, surprised by her question. In the vise before him is a wire foot.

"It's an all-purpose clothes hanger," he says.

"It scared me."

There's Richard's distracted half-smile and Isabel knows he has already stopped seeing her, that he's staring into the hallway and he isn't even seeing that. Is he plotting out an ankle, calculating where to joint the wires? Afraid she might fly apart from another gaze that goes right through her, Isabel makes her face flat and concentrates on his shelves of inventions: the long-armed claw for cleaning roof gutters without a ladder; those tiny brushes for dusting light switches; the screwdriver with a flashlight built into its handle. And there's another shelf she won't let herself look at, cluttered with little racing cars and horses made of tin cans that the children on the block love so much.

"There's nothing scary about it," Richard finally says, as if to himself. "It's a carry-on for big shots who don't like wrinkled suits. Even holds shoes and socks." He points to the five toe-like curves at the tip of the wire foot. His hand is still smudged with magic marker.

"Oh," Isabel says, but she doubts that anyone would ever want to buy that odd figure.

With another dinner over, Isabel sits with Richard on the living room couch in front of the TV, but she can't quite concentrate on the broad gestures of a flawless family negotiating some temporary crisis. Soon Richard gets up and walks to the kitchen, returns with nothing, then stands in the doorway again, his back to her, as if deciding where to wander next. When two telegenic children chase each other with carefree banter around a coffee table, she glances at the Horizontal dial: just a slight, destabilizing twist could stutter those actors down the screen helplessly, endlessly. Isabel shuts her eyes, imagines her own dizzy free fall.

There's a rush of laughter from the television and she opens her eyes, almost expecting to see Richard once again kneeling before her. He's standing in the doorway, facing the hall, and then he's gone, restless with something he isn't talking about. Isabel stands—she needs to hold that photo again and call up his shy unbuttoning.

The photos are in the box on her dresser now, though she can't remember putting them back. She riffles through the pile twice but can't make the picture appear. Could she have dropped it somewhere? She scans the carpet into each corner and peers at the dark under the bed, she opens Richard's closet and crawls among his scattered shoes until her head grazes against the wire figure's new foot.

Kneeling there, she pushes away his clothes and stares up at the slightly swaying thing. It's really just a cartoonish outline. Why would anyone want to fit clothes over something that looks so awkward? Isabel reaches out for one of the wire hands, examines the clumsiness of the circular palm and broad fingers. With some strain she manages to bend a metal curve into a recognizable thumb. Then she carefully squeezes the rest into tapered fingers and goads the palm into an oval. She places her own hand against the cool wire outline: it's a comfortable fit. Isabel stands up and moves back. Those thighs are too thin, the shoulders too squarish. Gripping the cold metal, she begins to press and pull.

That night Isabel lies in the darkness and tries to hold her eyelids open with her fingers, afraid she might dream another terrible dream of a vanishing baby. She tries listening to Richard's breathing, the occasional car going who knows where, but her fingers slowly slip down her cheeks until she's asleep.

Isabel dreams that her face fills the wire circle in the closet. She tries to call out to Richard but her lips won't move, and as she struggles to make a sound—a whisper, a cry, anything—jigsaw cracks streak across her stiff face. They widen until pieces tumble down: a flat shining cheek, a tip of chin, half of her mouth.

She wakes. It's still dark. She carefully makes her way down the stairs, to her dining room puzzle, and she dismantles that jigsaw face, its features crumbling in her hand. But hiding the pieces in a box isn't enough: clutching bits of ear, hair, lips, she takes them to the kitchen and stuffs them down the disposal. The kitchen fills with a grim and lovely gnawing, and Isabel lets it go on and on until the cabinets seem to shake.

During breakfast Richard is restless in his chair and throughout the morning he always seems just down the hall or in the next room, though maybe Isabel's only imagining this: when they were first married she often felt he was beside her even when he wasn't. And when he was, his silence was an invitation, a quiet asking. She stops, listens for his breathing, and the phone rings. Isabel almost jumps at the sound.

"Hi, 'Bel, it's Donna. Listen, could you cover me tonight? My little girl's got chicken pox—you wouldn't believe how fast it spread—and she's just itching so bad, poor thing. . . ."

Isabel doesn't want to hear any more. "I can do it," she breaks in. "What's your shift?"

"Three to nine. Hey, thanks."

"I'll be there," she says, even though she has to work a morning shift tomorrow.

When she puts down the receiver she hears sharp footsteps heading toward the workshop. Richard *was* nearby, listening. The door closes and Isabel knows he's shutting himself away from the fact that she has to work extra whenever he's laid off. When the bell-like clanging of the hammer begins she feels her own limbs ache. If she had a wrench or a screwdriver she'd range through the rooms and loosen the legs of tables and chairs, undo every doorknob and doorjamb. She escapes to the backyard, to kneel beside the flower beds and the week's weeding, yet she doesn't feel her usual pleasure from tugging at roots. She listens to the children's bicycle race circling around the block—there's Danny's whoop, that's Allie's teary shout.

Isabel stuffs humid green piles into a plastic bag and notices that the workshop banging has stopped—Richard must be upstairs now, attaching the last metal leg and foot. She wonders if he'll notice what she did to the figure. Then the porch door bangs and there are Richard's steps on the sidewalk—the beginning of the long walk he'll take until she's gone to work.

After watering the plants more than she should, Isabel finally goes back inside to prepare dinner and busies herself in the kitchen with the crock pot for Richard's stew. She arranges his place setting on the table, and when the fork and knife clink down beside the plate, Isabel pauses. What does that sound remind her of? She lifts the fork again and drops it two, three more times and listens to its tinny clatter—it's just like that wire figure upstairs when she first pulled it toward her. Yes, she realizes, she's alone in the house with it now. It's finally complete.

Isabel suddenly can't help wanting to see the thing and its finished foot. She walks softly up the stairs, past all the muted wooden creaks that seem like whispering, and enters the bedroom. Crouching in Richard's closet, she can make out the wire feet resting on the ground together, flat against the carpet. Dangling above them are her long white gloves, fit snugly over those wire hands.

She pushes away at Richard's shirts and sees a pair of her panties stretched like a flat empty pouch over the outline of the hips, her favorite bra strapped across the chest and hanging loosely. Isabel almost cries out at this distorted image of herself. Instead, with a curious finger she pokes one of the lace cups. It easily collapses inward. The figure shivers, as it must have when Richard dressed it, and Isabel retreats and fills her hands with her hair, pulling until her scalp aches, wishing she could rise into the air and fly away from such a thought.

A computerized voice intones the prices, total, and change while Isabel punches up stationery and blenders and videocassettes, but she barely listens. She keeps imagining Richard finding her photograph, staring at it until something opens up inside him, and then he searches through drawers of stockings and cotton nightgowns until he finds her white gloves. He holds them gently, fingers the smooth fabric until he's filled with that long-ago intimate moment. Finally he chooses panties from among the snug rows in a drawer. He pauses and pats them, takes in their pliant warmth, and then he reaches for a bra from a neatly folded pile.

Isabel rings up mouthwash, aspirin, and disposable diapers, and tries to remember what else she wore in that photo. Wasn't it high, dark pumps, a white blouse with padded shoulders? And a gray skirt, she's sure, a wool skirt that scratched against her knees. She knows she owns nothing like them now, so during her break Isabel searches through the circular clothes racks, turning from one disappointment after another. When she finds a white blouse with just the right shoulders and thin collar, Isabel holds it against her and tries to evoke Richard's shy fumbling, the precise distance between his fingers and her skin. But wasn't the fabric softer, weren't the white buttons rounded, not flat?

Isabel stands quietly in the dark foyer, a shopping bag under her arm. The living room lights are out. Though that long shadow on the couch might be Richard, Isabel can't force out even a whisper. I'll do this alone, she decides, and sneaks up the stairs.

In the bedroom she pulls the blouse from the bag, rips off the sales tag, and starts to undo the buttons. But before she can pad over to Richard's closet, she hears a creak of the floorboards out in the hallway. Then there's another—he must be just outside the door. Isabel quickly stows the blouse in her dresser. When she sees the shopping bag on the floor she kicks it under the bed, wincing at the noise, then turns and waits for her husband's entrance. But all she hears is silence—is he waiting for her? With a regretful glance back at the dresser—she'll have to leave that blouse for later—Isabel leaves the bedroom as nonchalantly as she can.

The hall is empty. She'd like to believe that creaking was just the house itself, but the door to the guest room is ajar. Again, she finds she can't call Richard's name, and she hurries downstairs.

In the kitchen Isabel opens the lid of the crock pot and sees that Richard must have spooned out a plate of stew for himself. Then she hears the faint wooden rasp of a drawer opening upstairs. The drawer closes, then another opens. It's Richard, and Isabel knows what he must be searching for. But will he recognize the blouse when he finds it? She waits, and through the lingering quiet comes the slide of his distant closet door.

Barely able to contain herself, Isabel is waiting below when Richard walks down the stairs. At the sight of her he stops in mid-step, and he looks so sheepish standing there, one foot suspended in the air, that Isabel feels herself suppressing a grin. Maybe they should both laugh right now, just as they laughed years ago—if only the television were on, some studio audience might get them going! But the house is quiet, the moment passes, and Richard takes his step. They both glance away as he walks past her to the dark porch.

Isabel follows. He's settled in his chair, facing the cool night breezes, and she sits nearby on the steps. Together they listen to the air sifting through the trees, the drone of a distant airplane hidden by clouds. Already this is a bit like their long-ago, silent moment, and neither of them has to say a word about the secret they're creating.

Isabel spends her lunch break the following day in the thrift shop, searching through cluttered aisles and brimming cardboard boxes. The hangers squeak, as if encouraging her to hunt further through the cotton prints, the long, dark skirts, and she feels a budding panic at the sight of other customers, afraid they might be the first to find what she's looking for.

In an old box behind a stack of lampshades, Isabel finds a pair of dark pumps. Though the left heel has a few ugly scuffs, she steps into the dressing room. The shoes fit, and Isabel sits for a long time in quiet gratitude. When she slips them off she remembers Richard kneeling before her, cradling her bare feet, and his hand is whole again—she can feel the long gentle touch of his index finger and thumb, and she waits for him to rise and unbutton her blouse. He hesitates, and so she shifts a little in her seat to encourage him, she reaches out to stroke his soft, straight hair. But the salesgirl is knocking on the door: "Honey, are you all right in there?"

When Isabel returns home, still held by that reincarnated touch, Richard is standing in the living room doorway, scanning the bag under her arm, its bulge. Afraid he'll reach for it with his bad hand, she walks by, yet feels the unfairness of this and stops by the stairs when he says, "Shoes?"

"Uh-huh," she replies, turning to him, "but they need a little polishing."

She knows Richard wants to offer his help—his hesitation is so familiar—so she sets the bag down by the banister. "I'll go make a quick dinner," she says.

Later, as she shakes the colander, steam rising from the spaghetti, she watches Richard's reflection in the darkened window before her: he's waiting at the table, his eyes following her. She lingers, filling the bowls—he can watch as long as he likes.

"So how was work?"

Startled by this unexpected question, Isabel pauses. If he's really curious, he's picked the right day. She places the spaghetti on the table and says, "Well, a fellow came in before closing and bought seven different kinds of lawn sprinklers. The girl at the next counter even noticed."

Richard laughs—he was actually listening.

"We couldn't imagine what he wanted with them all. I wish I'd asked."

Serving himself, Richard says, "Maybe the guy . . . oh, I don't know." He lifts his knife and fork, then stops and grins. "No, wait—maybe he's a spy. Maybe each sprinkler . . . is a different signal. For his contact. The kind that covers a whole front lawn means, 'I'm being watched.' Or one of those twisting jobs means, 'Meet me at the drop-off point.' Stuff like that."

Stunned by Richard's sudden burst of words, Isabel doesn't know what to say. "Yeah," he continues, twirling repetitive loops of spaghetti, "it might be a kind of sprinkler code. Big secrets—has nothing to do with the lawn. Better tell your manager to call the FBI." He stops, embarrassed by all this talk, and soon he's sopping up sauce with garlic bread—he seems surprised that the meal is so good.

That night, Isabel listens to Richard's stirrings in the dark and she can't wait for that figure in the closet to be finished. Then, she's sure, he'll reach across the space between them on the bed.

He'll whisper to her as he used to—first complaints about the assembly line, perhaps one of those little jokes she could never remember afterward, then short phrases about her hair, lips, shoulders, and his remembered voice murmurs to her until she falls asleep.

Two days later, Isabel is swinging the shopping bag in time to her light gait as she returns home, enjoying the heft of the folded woolen skirt inside. Even though she found it in an expensive shop and blanched at the price, her search is finally over!

She's halfway up the walk to her porch when she hears the squeal of an electric drill. With a few quick steps she stands just outside the workshop and tries to decipher that shrill grinding. What could Richard possibly be adding to the figure—a face? She opens the door. He's bent over the workbench vise, sparks rising as he drills a hole in a thin metal tube. There's curved piping of all sizes scattered across the bench. Richard turns his goggled face up, the plastic lenses hazy with tiny scratches.

"You gave me a great idea, hon," he says, smiling, and he gestures at the metal clutter. "I'm making a sprinkler—comes with attachments, so folks can water the lawn any way they like. Seven sprinklers in one, y'know?"

He picks up a slim, half-oval cylinder. "This one'll do the side lawn, but it won't drench the house or spill over into the neighbor's." He reaches for another. "And this one . . ."

"Not now, all right? Maybe later," Isabel says. She shifts the shopping bag from one hand to another, shakes it a little so he'll notice.

Richard nods, though she's not sure how well he can really see through those goggles. Or is he staring through her again? He turns back to the vise. She shakes the bag again until the skirt inside thrashes about—doesn't he understand what she's found? But the drill has already started its piercing whine. Sparks loop into the air.

She walks alone up to the bedroom. The drill squeals again.

Isabel slides open the closet door and pushes away Richard's shirts. The figure simply hangs there, the clothes flat on its frame, and Isabel is embarrassed at the sight of the panties beneath the blouse, the curve of those exposed wire thighs. She pulls the new skirt from the bag and presses its itchy woolen pile against her face, inhales the startling freshness of this last piece of a puzzle she and Richard have been trying to solve.

Then Isabel kneels down before the figure, gathers one wire foot and then the other, and slips them, jangling, into the gray skirt. When she pulls the skirt up the curve of wire legs the figure shivers, as if it too understands something momentous is about to occur. Isabel stops and shivers as well, imagining that it's ready to lift both arms and raise itself off the wooden rod, no longer content to dangle.

Isabel grabs the figure's hands to hold it still. She feels the wire edges through the gloves' fabric, the soft fabric that has no real fingers to cling to. *I* should be wearing these gloves, she thinks, and she pulls them off. The skirt, only halfway up those thighs, slips slowly to the ground. *So why stop?* Isabel decides, reaching for the buttons on the blouse, and within moments she's undressed the wriggling figure down to its bare metal frame.

The scattered clothes lie in a pile on the floor, and Isabel realizes with a shock that they're waiting for her. *Of course,* she thinks, and she strips off her outfit as quickly as she can. But when she stands exposed before that still quivering figure, its emptiness seems to mock her, its faint metal tinkling sounds like a dismissive giggle. "Don't," Isabel hisses, rage rising inside her, and suddenly she's ready to tear apart that torso, twist off that head. She shakes her fist at the thing, squeezing her hand so hard it trembles painfully before her, curled and floating.

Uncoiling her hand and stretching her fingers, Isabel watches the pink patches vanish from her palm. Then she reaches out and bends and bends a wire shoulder until she tugs an arm joint loose. But she cuts herself on a sharp metal edge and a red squiggle runs across her knuckle. She licks it. At first queasy at her own taste—

a slightly strange sweetness—she sucks at herself until no new drop appears.

She returns to that dangling arm, but when its cold metal edge brushes against her breast as if in protest, Isabel has to suppress a scream. She lifts the figure off the rod and throws the clattering thing on the rug. Kneeling, she bends and twists apart the wire limbs and body, and though some part of her cries out against this, it's a tiny voice, one that grows smaller and smaller, until the figure is nothing but a grimace of wires on the floor. Isabel stops, gulping for air. What will Richard say when he sees this? she thinks, What have I done?

"Just what I needed to," she says to the empty room. She kicks those misshapen pieces into the closet and slides the door shut. Then, with great deliberation, Isabel dresses herself in those clothes that are hers, hers.

She sits in a chair and assumes the pose of the photograph: her lips slightly parted, her eyes oval, her legs crossed and balanced just so, one foot stretched, the shoe pointing toward the door. Richard will forget he ever made that wire thing when he sees me, she thinks. But the door is still closed, there's no hint of him. Her legs begin to numb.

The drill downstairs screeches again and again, but he *has* to finish sometime. Then he'll wonder where she is. He'll have to remember her standing in the doorway holding that shopping bag, he'll understand at once what was inside and he'll be amazed that he didn't notice before. Isabel wants so much to hear the steps' little creaks and groans that she knows so well until there's just Richard's hesitation on the other side of the door, his fingers on the knob but not yet turning it, he's so excited. And when he finally opens that door he'll see her patient smile. Then, like a photo rising out of itself, Isabel will raise her arms, and each white-gloved hand will stretch toward him.

The Reverse

Still exhausted from hauling Happy Shrimp platters at the restaurant last night, Fern lingers in bed and listens to the muffled echo of David's voice in the shower. He's crooning a song he made up yesterday about a heart breaking into different geometric shapes, how unhappiness is only a puzzle with actual pieces that can join and heal. Fern loves the awkward quirks of his voice as he sings about a pulsating trapezoid fitting with a warm little parallelogram. She imagines him in his subway booth later in the day, selling tokens and melodically counting out change, waiting for a great song to finally strike.

Fern has an audition for a commercial this morning, but she's wary of yet another script holding secrets she'll probably never decipher. And today's audition sounds so peculiar, the trade listing simply announcing, *Dress for the role you prefer*. She reaches across the bed for the clock—9:22, less than an hour—and then hurries over to the bathroom. Shivering from the cold floor tiles, Fern stares in the mirror at her blurry face, her flattened brown hair. With a sigh she pushes away David's razor and shaving cream, certain that only the most inventive application of makeup can make her presentable this morning. Fern digs her fingers in her lopsided hair but she can't fluff it. She decides to join David in the shower.

"Hey hon," she says to his soapy back, and suddenly the swirl of water at her feet and the wet folds of the shower curtain give Fern a brief glimpse of last night's dream, something about a beach. She closes her eyes and tries to hold the image, but David has turned around and is making slippery patterns on her breasts. Her back against the wet tiles, Fern smells his hair with its scent of shampoo, and her sleek arms encircle him. Now I'm *really* going to be late, she thinks. "Isosceles triangle," he croons, his hands sliding down her stomach.

Fern stands at the edge of a large room among a crowd of actresses in costume: there's the Slinky Diet-Cola look, the All-Natural-Cereal look, the Harried Housewife look and more. Not sure why she's even come, Fern glances down at her plain blouse and jeans, thrown on in her rush: the Unprepared look.

Technicians are slowly swiveling large cameras into place. Why are there cameras? she wonders. Everyone is wandering about and no one seems in charge. A woman with an enormous comb in her thick hair passes Fern and trips over a cable. She falls to her knees, the comb clattering on the floor, and Fern watches it dangle from the woman's lobe by a long silver chain. It's an earring, Fern realizes—what is *she* supposed to be? A lanky man with a clipboard helps the woman snatch up the swaying comb. When she stands and whispers to him, he giggles and writes something in his pad.

Then Fern notices the woman's clothes are inside out: loose threads hang from her shoulders, the broad, inner seams of her blouse are exposed, and from her pants the hidden flaps of pockets hang like wide, pale tongues. The inside white label on her blouse seems to shine out. Fern steps closer and leans forward, wanting to read the instructions, but instead she's suddenly recalling her dream. She was nude and walking along a crowded beach, but no one noticed because her tan had somehow reversed. Her body was pale white except for one horizontal strip of brown across her hips that blended in with her pubic hair, and another tan line across her breasts that hid her nipples.

The woman is facing her. "Are you trying to read my label? I *so* much like curiosity."

Fern nods, unable to speak, certain that everyone around them is watching. She resists the impulse to cover her chest, her crotch.

"One hundred percent cotton. I'm all natural. And I like to be washed in warm water."

Like a guilty child, Fern nods again.

The woman eyes her carefully. "A bit bland. But I don't think you'll *film* bland. Your name is?"

"Fern . . ."

"My god, what a name!" the woman laughs. "You'll be perfect." The man beside her scribbles away.

They lead her through the crowd and Fern realizes this has been an interview of sorts. The woman whispers to her lanky assistant. "All right, everybody," he calls out, "we've found our girl. Time to go home." Fern is almost alarmed to hear this—she had begun to think of Happy Shrimp as a career.

"What the fuck was this all about, anyway?" someone shouts.

The woman turns to her assistant. "Mick, dear, would you turn that off?" He slips through the crowd, murmuring apologies.

She turns to Fern. "I'm Marjorie, your director du jour. Now Fern, I know this sounds a bit *unorthodox*, but we're going to improvise our commercial. And we're going to do it right now."

No script? Fern thinks, but she doesn't have time to be relieved, because before the last actress has gone, she is standing in front of a stark blue backdrop and the makeup man is already blushing her cheekbones. "Nothing fancy," Marjorie says, "just give her a touch-up." She waves her hand at the backdrop, but Fern can't turn to look. "Don't worry about all that nothing behind you. The deal is, a downtown artist will draw the background later. Then we program it into a computer and everything will get, ah, frisky. But you, my dear, come first."

Marjorie turns and slaps her palms against her dangling pants pockets and shouts, "Where's the love interest?" She turns and whispers to Fern, "He's a redhead. Think lots of kiss-kiss."

Within minutes the lights are on Fern and her costar, but there's nothing to work with, no set, no script, no product. "Get to know each other, kids," Marjorie calls out. "Don't mind us. Or the lights. Or the cameras."

The redhead's face is as blank as a plate. He must have been the worst at his audition, Fern thinks—maybe we've both been selected as a joke. She tries a sidelong grin as they draw closer, but when they embrace she can feel the knots in his stiff shoulders. His arms hang limp at his sides. But he's the same height and build as David, so Fern closes her eyes and runs her finger slowly down his spine.

"Hold it," Marjorie calls out.

"I'm sorry. I just thought that . . ."

"No, I *like* it," she says, out of her chair and striding toward them. "It's tender and sexy, and that's the kind of identification we need for a drain cleaner, which *is*, by the way, what we're selling here. When your finger slips down his back it gives a subliminal message of water running down a pipe."

Fern's chin still rests, idiotically, on the redhead's shoulder, and she can only stare at Marjorie, afraid to admit she was merely thinking about her boyfriend.

Marjorie steps back a moment. "I think we'll take a close-up of those fingers first, then one of your face." She takes the comb from her hair, the thin chain jangling, and brushes back Fern's bangs. "Keep your eyes closed first. And then open them so all our housewives at home can imagine what he's rubbing against you down there, okay?"

*　　*　　*

When they're finally done Marjorie shouts out, "All right, strike the set!" A few technicians laugh, and they gather up cords and lights.

"Thanks," the redhead whispers to Fern before walking off, and she stands alone, still not quite believing what has happened. Marjorie approaches, talking to Mick: "Remind Pascal again that I want the animation sloppy, not slick, okay?"

Then Marjorie is beside her. "Impressive. I knew *you'd* be the one to come through. Really, all I wanted from that fella was the back of his head, all those nice red curls. And now, dear, there are these little annoyances called forms . . ."

While Fern finishes signing, Marjorie asks, "So, do you always read other people's labels? Wait, don't answer that. Can I give you a lift?"

"Sure," Fern immediately says, though she'd rather take the subway and stop at David's station with the good news, tell him how he was her unseen partner. But Marjorie is already strolling away and Fern follows.

They walk up the block, the wind ruffling their hair. "So," Marjorie says, the stray strings of her exposed seams fluttering, "you want to know all about me. You've heard about Conceptual Art? Well, I invented Conceptual Radio. I deejayed for an early morning radio program I designed, called *Alarm Clock Music.* 'This show is a public service,' I'd whisper in a husky voice that really got the letters coming in, 'featuring music so awful it *makes* you get up.' I'd flip on the Rice Krispies Snap! Crackle! Pop! theme song arranged for string quartet—the scherzo version— and then segue into a piano roll made from the Braille version of Joyce's *Ulysses.* Ah, here's my car," she says. Fern is disappointed that it's an ordinary tan import.

They get in and Marjorie presses the lighter on the dashboard before driving off. "I woke up the whole city. Absenteeism was zip, the Chamber of Commerce threw a banquet in my honor. And then," she pauses, lighting her cigarette, "I quit." Marjorie shifts gears, silent, and Fern understands she's supposed to respond.

"Why?"

"Why, you ask? Never keep dancing while the termites are eating through the floorboards, I always say. Anyway, I hustled arts grants with the usual performance art scam. Finally I got this idea for a project on the American housewife, an adventure domestica in fifteen- and thirty-second installments, in collaboration with major corporate sponsors. I figured, what with cable, video rentals, CD-ROMs, and the Internet, it's clear the networks' ratings are going bow-wow, so we're at a point where anything is possible. And I was right, because you *know* a company's desperate if they hired me with complete creative control. Actually, they think they need a huge loss—all that computer stuff will *cost*, y'know—something that'll help them when they file for Chapter Eleven. Ha—just wait."

Fern is disappointed to see they're nearing her block. Now she just wants to listen and listen. Marjorie looks at her and grins. "You don't talk much, but you don't need to. Look, when I get an impulse, I follow it, and that's what you did today. Twice. But you didn't know it. Well, Fern, you're going to be my ordinary housewife with hidden depths."

Fern sits in her agent's office, waiting, wishing Marjorie wasn't so late. While Dougie reads the long-term contract Marjorie has offered, Fern glances at the walls and all the framed and signed photos of stars who seem to stare past her dreamily.

Dougie waves the pages at her. "You've read this carefully, Fran?"

Fern nods and doesn't correct him. Just a week ago he didn't return her phone calls.

Dougie takes off his horn-rimmed glasses and pokes them at the contract. "This is unortho, very unortho. No script, everything improv? Only one commercial per sponsor and you don't even know what you're selling until right before the first take?"

She wishes he wouldn't clip his words like that, it's so annoying, but Fern only stares at his pinched lips and says nothing.

There's more he could question—no outside work or interviews for the term of the contract—but she doesn't want trouble. She wants to sign.

He puts his glasses back on and sighs, his eyes larger as he stares at her silence. She can see he doesn't think this will fly at all. "But it *is* your first break," he says, "so I don't want to push too hard, she might change her mind." And when Marjorie finally arrives and sits before them Dougie only manages a lackluster, "Y'know, Fran and I have a teeny question about the interview clause . . ."

"Donnie, *Donnie,*" Marjorie says, "for this project to work we need to stay mysterious, *n'est-ce pas?* So no one gives interviews. Trust me, I know." She points to her earrings: little plastic garbage cans, the lids bulging up with bright refuse. "I can hear America singing."

Fern giggles.

"Don't," Marjorie says. "It's bad luck to laugh at earrings, didn't your mommy ever teach you anything?"

"Fern, Fern!" David shouts out, and she runs down the hall to the living room, in time to see herself in the center of the television screen. Her chin is resting on the redhead's shoulder, surrounded by a wild, animated kitchen: the edges of the cabinets and the refrigerator door are off-balance, almost ready to fly away, but Fern is the still, steady center.

As she watches the close-up of her large gleaming eyes, her little squiggle of a smile, Fern feels oddly fragile and she's glad when the commercial ends. But David has long anticipated his invisible influence in this little drama, and he slaps a blank tape in the VCR and he won't stop watching TV until her commercial finally returns. Then he can't stop replaying Fern's hand moving down that back, the widening of her excited eyes.

The commercial becomes hugely popular. Soon Fern stands again before another blue backdrop, facing the cameras. Marjorie saunters up to her wearing cut-off jeans over white panty hose, and there are stick figures painted on the bright nylon fabric, engaged in awkward intimate acts like some child's uninformed dream of sex.

Marjorie whispers, "Liquid cleanser." Then she sits back down by the cameras, her legs crossed. The raised arms of an ecstatic figure span her shin and one painted hand, spread across her knee, seems to be waving.

Everyone waits. Fern's own arm rises, her hand first circling in the air as if waving back, whether at that figure or at Marjorie, she's not sure. Then she's rubbing her palm against the air, scrubbing at a nothing that seems to surround her. She twists about, both hands now billowing, and she's surprised at how easy it is to move in an acrobatic, widening circle until whatever she's washing away is finally gone.

"My, my, some *great* close-ups," Marjorie calls out, and she walks over to Fern. "Now I'd like to work out some different angles." She turns suddenly, back to the cameras. "Mick, dear, would you be a good shadow and follow me?" He just stands there by her empty chair, staring furiously at his pad. But Marjorie doesn't see this, she is looking at Fern with admiration, and then she laughs, her lips round with pleasure. "This is just what the gals out there will like, they won't know what you'll do next."

Fern turns off the faucet and lets the plate slip into the suds. "What?" she asks.

"I said if that wasn't enough . . ." David sips his beer and leans back in his chair, "this old guy jumps the turnstile—he can barely do it—and the cop on the beat chases after him. And 'cuffs him. An *old* guy." David looks at the ceiling, sips some more. "And then some turd mouths off because I won't take a Canadian quarter."

Fern goes to him and tickles his knee with her damp fingers. "Poor sweetie, how are you ever going to write your great song with rotten days like this? I'm sure tomorrow will be better."

But David is in one of his moods: he cups an ear and mouths a silent response, as if he's still inside his glass booth. Then he wanders down the hall and hums aimlessly, jiggling coins in his pocket—his usual rhythm section—but he can't seem to find an opening into a new melody.

Eventually he joins Fern on the couch and watches TV: two fat people wisecracking over a smoking barbecue grill. The laugh track laughs and then on the screen an acrobatic Fern is scrubbing away a malevolent cloud of grime.

David rushes to the VCR and presses the Record button. He catches her last elastic movements as the bedraggled, illustrated kitchen around her becomes almost painfully pristine. "Jeez, what gave you the idea to do that?" David asks, pressing Rewind.

Fern hesitates, wishing she had another romantic tale to tell him. "You," she says, surprising herself. "I imagined we were washing each other in the shower."

David watches a few seconds of the replay and then he shouts, "Okey do*key!*" He jumps up and dances with Fern's peculiar scouring motions on the screen.

The phone rings and Fern gets it. "Hello, doll," Dougie says. "I think I can get you a spot on Letterman."

"But Dougie, no interviews, remember?"

"What interview? There's no interview. He just makes fun of you for five minutes."

Fern hears David pacing in the hall, jangling coins again. "I'm just not sure it's possible," she says.

"You're worried about that wacky contract you signed, right?"

"*We* signed."

"Who knew, who knew?"

Fern can hear David singing. "Don't scrub the floor, scrub me," he begins. It's his first new song after a month of silence.

"Dougie, look, I have to go, okay? Bye." She listens to the unpredictable wavering of David's voice, and she's pleased that her little lie has made him so happy.

*   *   *

Fern is soon accustomed to finding her accomplished domestic face on TV, in the center of animated kitchens of nervous color and edgy chiaroscuro. *Artforum* runs a review of her latest commercial and hails New Wave Domesticity. *TV Guide* reports that housewives buy whatever Fern sells, just so the spots will continue to run. Dougie keeps calling to tell her that *People* will be happy to proclaim her the National Housewife, if only she'd grant an interview. Fern is glad she can't. She doesn't feel very housewifely, even after devouring women's magazines, memorizing newspaper recipes, and trying to learn knitting.

She clicks away with her long needles during afternoon soaps, but the repetitive weaving of her hands lulls her too easily. She looks up at the television: a glamorous blonde hides a letter behind a sofa pillow just as a lushly handsome man enters the room. He greets her and sits down right where the letter is hidden. His thin smile defies interpretation as he stares into the camera. The music swells.

Then Fern's face is in close-up, her features filled with sudden surges of twitches and grimaces, while behind her is yet another animated background: a succession of homey meals prepared by invisible hands. The sound track is the grunt of the dishwasher, the groan of the vacuum cleaner and the drunken whoosh of the clothes dryer, and every image and sound seems to change with each new flicker of pain on Fern's face, until she reaches for a floating bottle of aspirin.

Fern sets down her tangle of yarn and glances about her living room. If only I could make *this* writhe around me, she thinks. But I'm just a lucky fraud. She scrunches her face, warps her lips at the inflexible furniture, and the phone rings.

"Doll? I've got a bit part for you on 'Home Improvement,' and it's just the beginning—"

"Dougie, you *know* I can't." She contorts her cheeks and buckles an eyebrow at the all-too-solid coffee table.

"Doll. It's time to renegosh."

"Please, I don't want to jeopardize—"

"Okay okay okay. Remember, when you're ready, I'm ready."

"I know." Fern says good-bye, and she looks down at the confusing knot of her unfinished sweater. The phone rings again and Fern hesitates before picking up the receiver, she's had enough nagging. But it's Marjorie.

"Fern? We have a shoot lined up for tomorrow morning—sorry it's such short—"

"That's okay," Fern says. She pauses. "Uh, Marjorie?"

"I'm still here."

"I'd like to push myself more. How about telling me ahead of time what's up so I can prepare?"

"*Prepare?* I don't know, kiddo, we're doing so well the way we—"

"You're probably right," Fern sighs. "It's just that I had this impulse—"

"An *impulse*. Well, why *not* take a chance? How about I give you a teeny hint?"

Fern grins into the receiver. "Let's hear it."

"Tomorrow you'll have a costar. Female, and *much* younger than you."

"How much younger?"

"Oh, don't you want even a little surprise?"

After saying good-bye Fern wants to treat herself to the biggest piece of chocolate she can find. She walks to the grocery around the corner, and in a cramped aisle of sweets she notices a graying woman peering intently at boxes of pudding on the shelf. Fern stops: it's a pudding she did a spot for. She remembers how a spoonful of vanilla transformed itself into enticing, shivery shapes in front of her continually amazed face.

The woman hesitates, her nail tracing the spoon on the cover of one of the boxes, but then she grabs it and drops it in her cart. How often do I hold that spoon in her mind? Fern wonders. She follows the woman to the checkout counter, then out the door and behind her on the crowded sidewalk. Fern imagines that she's somewhere inside everyone walking by her, multiplied like the repeated images in a row of department store TVs. And where do

I go when they stop thinking of me? A bit woozy at this thought, she stops at the edge of the park and sits down on a bench. Fern closes her eyes, and through the dull hum of traffic she hears the distant sound of laughter in the park. A girl's laughter. That could be my *costar,* Fern thinks.

She follows the voice, each new happy burst leading her to a shaded clearing. A young mother lies on the grass while her daughter squirms all over her, transforming her into a shield, a ladder, a cushion. The mother seems to be snatching ten, fifteen seconds of sleep at a stretch. The girl awkwardly slaps her palms together: "Clap hands! Clap hands!" she sings out, her face alive with delight. Fern watches carefully and cups her hands around her eyes, creating a screen around them. *Aha,* she thinks—whatever I'll be during tomorrow's shoot, I'd better be tired.

When Fern returns to her apartment she stands in the living room and tries to imagine a little girl at her side. What should they do together, and with what product? If only Marjorie were marching toward her, about to divulge the secret. Fern strains to hear whispered words that don't come, and when she turns to the darkening window she can only see herself.

Watching her reflection, she reaches her hand out, as if squeezing the shoulder of a child beside her. Pretending her knuckles are tickled by the girl's long hair, Fern twirls a finger at an imagined strand. Then she hears David at the door, the bolts unlocking, and he's walking down the hall, swinging an air freshener by its string. "Just one sniff and you'll be mine," he sings. He nuzzles Fern's neck, and her almost invented child fades to nothing.

Over dinner, while Fern tries to concentrate on the empty chair she's pulled up to the table, David scats "Gimme gimme good margarine." Later, his hands in the soapy sink, he serenades the stacked plates in the dish drainer with "Let's dry off together tonight," and he looks over his shoulder for her approval. Fern almost asks him to stop, but hesitates. Even if they *do* sound too much like jingles, she can't help feeling pleased that she's inspired David to create all these new songs.

That night, with her musical David finally asleep, Fern lies beside him and again tries to conjure up the girl. What might a child want, so lonely in her own room—a glass of water? What might be keeping her awake—a strange sound in the toy chest? Or perhaps the carpet has come alive under the night light, making strange, barely visible ripples. But instead of hearing a girl's pleading voice, Fern is filled with the thought of the rug under her own bed, its woolen weave disentangling itself, wriggling ominously and ready to reach out at the foot of anyone foolishly considering escape.

Fern crouches exhausted before the camera and, searching for an idea, she tangles her hand in the blonde hair of the little girl standing beside her. But the child can only offer a precociously well-choreographed smile and wait, and all of Fern's inspiration is on the other side of sleep.

Marjorie quickly calls off the shoot and sits beside her in a corner. "Did we overprepare last night? A mistake, perhaps." She shakes her head and her earrings, two bright plastic sailboats, bobble and sway. "Oh, storm-tossed waves!"

Fern says nothing; her jaw hurts from stifling so many yawns.

"Okay," Marjorie says, and her fingernails flick at the air, as if any difficulty can be easily brushed aside, "we can continue in the afternoon. In the meantime, why not a little nappy? You can crash in my apartment."

So ashamed of her failure, Fern can't even look at Marjorie. "I think I'd rather go back to my place, thanks."

"Compromise. A drive home." Marjorie isn't asking.

In the car they're both silent. "Hey," Marjorie finally says, "you think you have troubles? Haven't you noticed that Mick isn't around any more? We broke up."

"You and Mick? You were . . ."

"Yeah yeah. He wasn't much, believe me, but I don't like being dumped." She pushes in the cigarette lighter with a deft slap of her palm. "Could you open the glove compartment, please?"

Fern pulls on the tiny door. Inside are cans of imported cocktail sausages.

"I'm absolutely starved. Would you be sweet and open one?"

Fern pulls the tab and lifts off the aluminum top. The sausages are packed together in a viscous gelatin and she struggles to pull one out.

Marjorie pushes Fern's hand away and expertly lifts a sausage from the thick goo. The cigarette lighter pops back with a click. Her knees balancing the wheel, Marjorie pulls out the lighter and presses its red coil against the sausage. Fern hears sizzling.

Marjorie eats the singed tip. "Revenge and protein, all at once. Want some?"

Fern shakes her head no at the acrid smell and looks away.

They're at her block. Marjorie scribbles on a piece of paper. "Look, just in case you lose the keys to your apartment—here's my address."

That afternoon, still under the spell of the odd hum that lingers after a nap, Fern hugs the little girl too tightly before the cameras, wanting so hard to possess the motherly moment that eluded her last night. This is the scene that David later can't help but gape at in front of the TV: in a photorealistic kitchen that is alarmingly antiseptic, a daughter tucked in a mother's enveloping arms reveals the urge to pull away when her smile erupts into a fleeting wince. But Fern won't break her grip. David presses the Rewind button and starts it again.

"I pretended you were leaving me," Fern lies, anticipating David's question, "but I wouldn't let you go."

David pulls away from that startling hint of secret distress flickering on the screen and turns to Fern. He grins and then walks slowly toward her, his arms outstretched in reconciliation. Laughing, he clutches and swings her around, and the apartment becomes a dizzy backdrop for the story she just made up. "How could I go when the floor shines so?" he sings, and Fern flinches in his twirling embrace.

*   *   *

Fern rushes toward the camera, her hair uncombed, her eyes puffy and slightly wild. She holds her hands up to her unsettled face. She is remembering her dream: returning from work, she discovers David's clothes on the couch, arranged as if he had just disappeared. His shirt is stuck against the back cushion, the empty sleeve resting on the armrest, and the legs of his jeans hang down off the couch to the carpet, his hollow socks nestled in and dangling from his shoes. She pokes among his clothes and finds his underpants, slightly soiled. She feels the irresistible urge to do a wash, and as she gathers up his clothes she feels something crawling in them and realizes it must be David, tiny and naked. She drops the bundle.

"Terrific," Marjorie says, "we'll keep that."

Fern blinks at the lights.

That evening over take-out Chinese, David humming his latest little ditty across from her, Fern is certain she knows what the new commercial will eventually look like: she'll be menaced by something like Unsightly Kitchen Mold, her mouth will be half-open in horror while the shadows of tentacles shift across her face. It seems so predictable now. With her chopsticks she picks a Szechuan peppercorn away from the Cashew Chicken and she deliberately chews on it, hungry for a nice sharp ache.

"Paper plates are flavor-mates," David is suddenly singing.

Not again, Fern thinks, looking up, and she breaks in. "Would you like to hear about today's shoot?"

David nods and waits expectantly, now back to humming. She wishes he would stop that, and so she decides to tell him the truth about her latest improvisation.

"I was *how* small?" he asks, leaning back in his chair.

"Well, I'm not sure . . ."

"And you *dropped* me? I mean, like I was a quarter or something, you just dropped me?" His face is stricken with disappointment.

Fern won't reply. She slips another pepper into her burning mouth.

Later, David sits before the TV, the sound off, and runs through all those performances he's taped, performances he thinks he's inspired. Fern stands in the doorway of the darkened living room, watching, and what she sees is a guilty hodgepodge of all those false stories she's told him. Then David is pushing buttons and her arms flap in fast-forward through an agitated laundry room, until David presses the Pause and Play buttons back and forth so that she's creeping in slo-mo toward a basket of dirty clothes a century away. Then she's hurtling backward, emotions rushing in reverse in fits across her face too fast to translate. Before David can press another button Fern leaves the room.

For a long time Fern lies in bed alone and in the dark. But she can still see, at the bottom of the door, those staggering flashes of TV light, waves and waves of it. Why won't he stop? She buries herself under the blankets. "I'm drowning!" she calls out, hoping to draw David away.

She waits. Nothing. "I'm drowning!" she shouts again, louder. Peering through the thin weave of the blanket, she can see David finally standing in the doorway, and she knows he is watching her shifting, covered form. She lifts a hand above the blankets: three fingers extended, going down for the last time, and after her last muffled cry she hears him pad across the room. She feels him pull the blankets to the edge of the bed until she is exposed before him, but Fern keeps her eyes closed: she wants so much to believe she's landed safe on the beach and that the sun is so bright, the sand so warm.

The next morning Fern crouches before the dark screen of the television, the videotape of her performances in her hand. It feels so light, so unmenacing, but she can't bear the thought of seeing her images go awry again. She slips it in the VCR, pushes the Erase button, and the tape whirs and whirs inside. Fern is glad David is far away on his rush hour shift, because as she disappears from the tape she realizes in one breathless moment that she never wants to see him, she never wants to *hear* him again. Fern plops down on the carpet, her sudden sadness exquisite, and she cries oddly pleasurable tears, her hands fisting in the thick pile until she remembers David's song about the vacuum cleaner that loves the taste of dirt.

She stands up as the disembodied lilt of his voice seems to rush at her. She hurries down the hallway, but from the bathroom she hears his jingle about the private pleasures of washing the tub. In the kitchen she leans against the counter, her hands to her ears, and she sees her unhappy reflection in the toaster. Again there is David's voice: "Put me in the toaster, honey, and I'll get hot for you, hot for you . . ." Fern can't help herself, she places her hand against that cool silver surface and imagines bread browning inside, the heat intensifying, but she can't remove her hand and the escaping smoke of burnt toast mingles with the smell of her own scorched flesh.

Fern shakes her head, trying to erase David's jingles. And that's all they'll ever be, Fern realizes, he won't ever find his great song because there isn't one in him. She can see David behind the glass booth: an express train rumbles by and his face merely mouths lyrics no one can hear while he handles coins, the tips of his fingers soiled with the images of national monuments and dead presidents. Then she imagines his fingerprints all over the apartment, those invisible stains over everything.

She rushes to the closet for furniture spray and returns to the living room with a rag. The phone rings and she lets it, too busy rubbing down an end table, and she listens to her recorded voice explaining that she's not in right now, and then after the beep she hears Dougie. "*Doll*, a call from *Altman*, he *loves* your stuff, wants to consider you for his next pic. You could improv your role. Listen, he wants to set up a *private* audition. Oh, I'm so glad you're not there to argue. Listen—we're talking movies, flicks, films, *motion pictures.* So what's a little breach of contract prob? Oh, I'm glad you're not there to argue. Think. Call. Bye."

Oh *god*, Dougie, so typically ambitious, Fern thinks. But she has stopped polishing, and she stares at herself across the room on the blank TV screen. She lifts the spray can and her tiny image does the same. Fern imagines behind that distant figure a stark blue background, and then she knows she's in her own commercial. The camera moves in: her face looks haggard, and there's a hint of that slight squinch she makes with her mouth. She seems oddly pleased with herself and she begins to speak.

"I threw the stinker out. He took all of his stuff, and now only his fingerprints are left. But not for long." She sprays the table, and then rubs it down very carefully with a cloth while staring at the camera. It zooms in until only Fern is on the screen: only her face, her bitter smile.

"Girls, are you like me? Upset that your ex has left his grimy marks all over the place? Then use Spray Away, and wipe him out of your life forever." She pauses. "It puts a nice shine on furniture, too."

Fern stands before her reflection on the blank screen and she lingers there for a long and satisfying moment: her commercial is over, and she did it alone. Marjorie will be so proud. Fern just *has* to tell her, and she searches in a drawer for a crumpled address.

"What a surprise," Marjorie says, opening her door, "what a pleasure: you've come to see my new earrings." A tiny triceratops sways from one ear, a stegosaurus from the other. "I love being surrounded by extinct creatures. Survivor's prerogative, no? So c'mon in." She waves a hand, her cigarette a smoky wand.

Fern enters and sees a *Bless This Home* sampler hanging framed over the TV, plastic slipcovers on a bright yellow couch, little ceramic squirrels and frogs holding poses on a knick-knack shelf. Fern stares at one of the figurines—a cat in apron, paw to mouth as if summoning a rowdy brood of kittens. This is not at all what she expected.

Marjorie laughs at her stunned face. "Don't look so shocked. This is my shrine to the American housewife's most average interior. I call it Necessity of Escape." She sits on her couch's squeaky slipcover, she leans over the coffee table and stubs her cigarette into an ashtray shaped like a toaster. "Really, it's taken you much too long to visit." She pats the cushion beside her. "Come sit, tell me what's brought you here."

Fern tries to settle comfortably on the stiff plastic cover. When Marjorie leans back patiently against flowery needlepoint pillows, Fern is suddenly struck with stage fright. Uncertain how to begin, she picks away at the clear plastic as if she could scratch through to the vivid fabric.

"Hey, don't be nervous," Marjorie says. She reaches for that anxious hand and squeezes the fleshy rise of Fern's palm.

Fern stops scratching the slipcover. But Marjorie is now lightly stroking her wrist and Fern watches, surprised at such a feathery touch, how shivery it makes her feel. Then Marjorie is whispering, "Oh, my," and her fingers trace the pattern of blue veins, the delicate bones on the back of Fern's hand.

"Don't be shocked," Marjorie murmurs, but Fern isn't, and she lets Marjorie pull her across the cushions—it seems like their own slow, dreamy close-up. She eases into Marjorie, feels fingers brush against her breasts, and when their mouths join Fern loses herself in the fluttery touch of their tongues.

Finally Marjorie breaks away gently. "Well, I guess we could say this has been a long and unusual courtship, no?"

Still a bit breathless, Fern nods. "Uh-huh," she manages, then she reaches out and squeezes Marjorie's knee.

Marjorie grins and reaches out for the buttons on Fern's blouse, but Fern shifts away slightly. "Y'know, there *is* something I came to tell you."

Marjorie leans back and shakes her dinosaurs. "I'm all ears."

Fern flicks off a shoe and tickles Marjorie's ankle. "I had this idea," she begins, and then she's describing her commercial, but before she can get to that last close-up of her bitter smile, Marjorie starts to laugh. "Oho, no need to go any further. It's brilliant, for sure. But dangerous—you just can't break your role as housewife like that, at least not so openly."

"Dangerous?" Fern gapes. "Why?"

"Why? Because all those reviews and articles about you, all that trash is wrong. You're really quite terrible at playing a house-wife . . . and that's the secret of your success." There's not even the tiniest smile on her face, she's absolutely serious.

"W-what do you mean?" Fern stammers, "I'm doing a great job. . . ."

"Exactly, honey, just not the job you think." Marjorie twirls an earring. "Your impulses aren't ordinary, you're not domesticated at all—just the reverse. Why do you think I chose you?"

Fern doesn't know what to say, but Marjorie isn't waiting for a reply. "Look, sweets, think about why we have all that animation. We add the background later so that even though on screen you're in a kitchen, something about your body language stays rootless, *capice?*" She strokes Fern's knee. "All those bored gals watching can sense that you don't really fit in there, and so they can sit at home and imagine that they don't really fit in either. There's a secret part of themselves that needs to believe this. If you were truly a hausfrau they'd switch the channel."

Fern sits there in her own silence. She starts ticking her nails at the plastic slipcover again, a rhythmic, rasping sound that reminds her of the whir of those erasing performances. If only she could make Marjorie's words vanish, but Marjorie keeps mur-muring. "Your idea is a *little* too over the top. Remember, the ten-sion between housewife and not-housewife has to be finely balanced. Ambiguity is everything, or else our lucrative gig is blown. And we wouldn't want that, would we?"

Her voice sounds so soft that Fern finds herself quietly nod-ding, she wants to agree, and when Marjorie says, "You'll always be my actress with hidden depths," Fern closes her eyes and the darkness becomes her own blank screen. She imagines this couch is just a stage, that Marjorie really didn't mean what she said and they're simply acting out a scene of two new lovers about to rec-oncile. She feels a gentle tug at her wrist.

"I hope you'll forgive me my little secret," Marjorie whispers, starting to draw Fern back. "It was touching to see you take everything so seriously, but you were doing so well it just wasn't necessary to fill you in."

So that's what I am, Fern thinks, the clueless star? Her face flushed, she pushes Marjorie away.

"Oh sweets, don't be upset," she coos, but Fern shrinks from her condescension, so terribly disappointed. How can she ever work with Marjorie again?

Marjorie leans closer, her face framed by those dangling dinosaurs, and then Fern sees her revenge: survivor's prerogative. Yes, she decides, this *is* a scene, but we're not alone. A camera crew is filming us, and Altman is sitting in the director's chair, waiting for me to improvise . . . and since this is my own private audition, there's no need to fill in Marjorie.

Fern fills her face with longing and, surprised at her quick calculation, says, "I'm a little . . . shy. Just give me a minute alone to collect myself . . ."

"You wait here," Marjorie murmurs, "I'll be right back," and she slips off to the bathroom, leaving Fern with the shelves of knick-knacks, the doe-eyed children framed on the walls, and a cigarette still smoldering in the ashtray. Fern supposes the camera crew, anticipating a nude scene, is ready to check the lighting for her small breasts and long legs when she stretches over the length of the couch. But there will be no nude scene. *This* will be more interesting, she thinks, leaning toward the ashtray, a nice surprise for Mr. Altman, and this time I know exactly what I'm doing.

Pushing the cigarette stub aside, she pokes her fingers into the ashes. Then she taps dark prints over the coffee table, and after smudging her fingers again she dabs ten ashy ovals across the brittle slipcovers of the couch. Fern regards her grimy patterns with satisfaction. She stalks the room and stains the faces of a few figurines, leaves a thumb smear on the quaint door of the quaint house of the framed sampler on the wall. Marjorie had better have a very good cleaning spray.

In the bathroom, the toilet flushes. Fern realizes she doesn't

have time to finish, but it doesn't matter. Altman has already settled back in his chair, impressed.

   She hears water running in the sink, Marjorie humming expectantly. My grand exit, Fern thinks, wiping her sooty hands
together, *Catch it, boys.* The hushed crew pivots the camera as she
strides away, and she's sure she'll get the part. She slips out the
front door, quickly clicks it behind her, and runs exhilarated
down the hallway, alone, alone. Pushing the button for the elevator, she listens to its muffled rumble rising up too slowly. She
presses the button again and again, and when the elevator finally
arrives with a silky whoosh, its door glides open like a curtain and
Fern steps in.

Geology

Standing beside the drilling equipment, Linda stared at herself in the mirror, unable to believe that her uniform was still brilliantly white. The morning and afternoon had been a succession of endless teeth cleanings—plaque and more plaque—that the dentist couldn't be bothered with, and she wasn't able to comfort today's frightened, teary child any more than she could yesterday's frightened, teary child.

Linda washed her hands, preparing for the last patient—another cleaning—though she really wanted to wipe her wet fingers across her uniform and leave long, moist stains. Instead, she imagined she was already back home in her apartment, the nape of her neck damp from a hot bath.

But she was still at work, surrounded by the dental school diplomas that covered the walls. The only exception was a landscape print: a forested hill that sloped to an open, grassy field, with mountains and an approaching bank of clouds in the background. As she listened to the muffled sounds of drilling in the next room, Linda wished the scene before her was a window instead, so something could change, so that even a single leaf might move. When she was a child and her parents forbade her to venture outside to the dangers of invisible germs, Linda often stood by a window and watched the world pass by. But now everything around her remained suspended in a bright, unchanging light. The fluorescent bulb in the hallway hummed its familiar hum, and Linda was briefly anxious that she might never move again and would remain in this office forever.

She heard a man's cough and turned around. The last patient of the day. How long had he been watching her? He smiled pleasantly, though Linda knew from experience what alarming surprises could hide within an ordinary mouth.

"Come in," she said, pretending she wasn't annoyed. He flopped down easily on the chair and fit his head between the rest pads. She dried her hands and took his folder from the files. He was a Mr. Henry Brown. Linda held his X rays to the light and let her eyes linger over them: except for a few fillings, his teeth were perfect, so straight and well proportioned. Thinking he might be watching her again, she glanced back at him. But he was sitting patiently, scanning the landscape print on the wall.

She began mixing the gritty cleaning paste, enjoying its thick, good smell, when he spoke. "That field—the one in the print you like so much?—it's in the middle of a transform boundary."

So he *had* been spying, Linda thought. "Excuse me?"

"That field in the print is right where two continental plates are shearing past each other. I'm a geologist, and that sort of country fascinates me. See those trees? Every year they're a couple of inches farther north."

"They move?" Linda put down his X rays.

"Well, the ground they're on moves. In about twenty thousand years that forest should be in the center of the picture."

"Really?"

"Except by that time, after hundreds of generations, they'll probably be different trees."

"Different trees," Linda said.

"But by then there will have been a number of local earthquakes, so there might not be any forest at all. Maybe an inland sea instead."

Linda looked up at the familiar print, now ripe with possibilities. It could never be the same again. Then she looked down at him, and somehow her heart fell right out of her, onto the metal tray filled with various picks and drill heads. "Tell me more, Mr. Brown."

"Call me Hank," he said.

She scraped around the edges of his teeth with a curved pick, and when she cleaned it with a paper towel from the tray, he slipped the suction tube from his mouth and told her he traveled a lot, doing energy and mineral research, though personally he was most interested in closing gaps in the fossil record. Linda took care to be gentle around his gums. The less he had to rinse his mouth and spit out pink water while she cleaned her pick, the more he could talk about unconformities and the pleasure of filling a fossil mold. And when Linda eventually finished with his teeth, at first she said nothing and pretended to examine his charts. She waited until he was in the middle of explaining the complicated breakup of Gondwanaland into lesser land masses, and then she announced that the cleaning was done.

"Oh, I wish we had more time," Linda said while he carefully moved his tongue over his teeth, "I'm so curious about where those other continents will drift to."

On their first date, Hank drove them along a cliff outcropping that had once been part of an ocean bed. Instead of flowers, he presented her with all of geologic time: he waved his hand, the other on the wheel, and said, "There was a sea here millions of years ago. If we were walking then, we'd be under water."

"Close the windows!" Linda laughed, and they quickly turned the handles.

"Look at that fish," Hank said, pointing out at the road. "Pure Devonian."

"Where?" Linda asked. Hank described the heavy, fishy jaw, the glittering, silvered armor of the fish he said floated alongside them, and she too began to see it through the watery murk, glad that the ancient fish swam outside. They were driving through a deep valley with trees of thick green, and Linda imagined the branches swaying beautifully like anemone. But it was a hot summer day, and with the windows up they began to sweat. "What will this valley be in the future?" Linda asked.

"A flat plain, most likely, with alluvial deposits you could sink your teeth into."

"How lovely." Feeling a wet trickle under her shirt from underarm to waist, she added, "Let's open the windows for a better view."

The suck of the rushing wind from the descending glass sounded like the air nozzle at the dentist's office. Not wishing to be reminded of work, Linda sang out, "Foraminifera! Orthohombic, amphibole, cephalopod!" and her lips enjoyed the motions of these new words Hank had taught her.

"Hey," he said, "you really *do* like this stuff, don't you?"

She nodded, and they continued to drive through familiar landscapes that Hank transformed before her eyes. This river, those hills wouldn't be there in twenty million years. That field was once a shoreline. Linda couldn't hear enough of these strange upheavals.

After their day of driving, Hank came up to her apartment and demonstrated exfoliation. Explaining how natural forces could peel off slabs of rock from exposed surfaces, he put his hand under her blouse. Linda closed her eyes and could feel his fingers against her belly, the bottoms of her breasts. "Alternating temperature changes," he whispered, "can loosen large flakes of rock." He began to undo buttons, adding, "Then, with the release of pressure, they slip off, revealing another level." The hooks of her bra released, and his hands moved down to her skirt.

*   *   *

Linda's long days as a dental hygienist would never be the same. Now that Hank had shown her the world was a vast collection of secrets that could be revealed, the dry sameness and stillness of the office was gone. Each mouth before her was now a landscape of change. A child's new, small teeth had once been only pink gums, ready to push open; a plaque-covered molar, ripe for decay, would eventually be pulled. She found herself so taken with these possible futures and pasts that she flooded one patient's mouth with the water nozzle, scraped another's raw nerve with her wandering pick, and Dr. Palen twice criticized her for preparing filling paste incorrectly. Still, Linda was proud that she too could see the invisible.

One day, they drove through a long cluster of hills on the way to see a glacial lake. One of the hills had been blasted open for the highway to pass through, and each sheer side was an exposed face of rock, angled in crazy contours from past cataclysms. "We call this a road cut," Hank said, pulling off to the side. "Millions of years are uncovered here." He took a small hammer from the glove compartment and grinned. "We are now in geologist's paradise."

Linda looked up at the straight, high face of rock, so beautiful and exposed, yet it all seemed oddly twisted and about to fall upon them in solid waves. Her face was pressed against the window and, though frightened, when she turned to Hank she said nothing. He hesitated, then put his hammer away. "Well, maybe next time," he murmured, and started the car. Linda was surprised by his understanding, and she wondered if he could also see how much was revealed in the simple gesture of her hand resting on his shoulder as they drove along.

The wedding was a small affair. Hank's mother and father weren't invited—the few times he ever mentioned his parents he called them The Scene of the Crime. Linda's distant parents didn't manage to show up, though they did call to congratulate her and complain of their many small ailments. They even promised to visit someday. But Linda couldn't quite imagine them in her new, small house, so extensively decorated with Hank's collection of rocks.

She was so happy in these rooms where Hank playfully stalked her, where chunks of trilobite-encrusted shale, polished granite that was once burning magma, and hollow geodes lined with crystals faced out from glass cabinets and shelves. At night they played Lava Flow. Hank illustrated this geologic phenomenon with his tongue, beginning at Linda's toes. Once, under his moist advance, Linda suddenly remembered how, a week before during a routine teeth cleaning, a middle-aged patient had licked her gloved and probing fingers. She had paused, startled, and as the man stared up at her, the tip of his tongue still stroking her fingertips, she quickly found a small cavity and pressed on it with her metal pick. He stopped. Neither of them spoke, and after he left, she had washed his saliva from her gloves with great deliberation before throwing them away. Wanting to forget this now, Linda pushed toward her husband, her head against the pillows, and Hank extended his hands to the curve of her spine. "Your back," he said between licks, "is as beautiful as any sedimentary anticline." She arched her back, pretending she was buried strata urging upward.

Three months later, Linda was pregnant. At work, as she stood in the dentist's office watching the leaves in the landscape print turn autumnal colors before her, she contemplated with quiet relief her coming leave of absence. Her own body was now a new landscape, her nipples darkening, her uterus expanding with small tremors, and at home she read books on fetal development, eager to anticipate each hidden transformation. Turning the pages, Linda secretly believed that all of evolution was inside her: an amoeba-like speck was slowly developing appendages until it would finally curl, fantastically, into a human being.

In Linda's sixth month, Hank reluctantly went on an extended field trip in the West, where he was put in charge of explosives.

He called to tell Linda how safe it really was to set off little artificial earthquakes and then track the shock waves to find hidden oil deposits. She assured Hank how relieved she was, but a sudden, sharp kick inside frightened Linda so much she almost dropped the receiver. When Hank's distant voice spoke to her of reservoir rocks and permeable beds, Linda closed her eyes and, because she had learned from geology that everything unseen can ultimately be recovered, she imagined him home, his slim frame appearing in the middle of an opened doorway.

But Hank didn't return early. One afternoon, as she sat snug with her wide belly in a living room chair, about to open Hank's latest letter, Linda suddenly felt she was waiting in a dentist's reception room for a long-delayed appointment. Anxious for her husband's return, she began imagining his features through their unborn child. She spent hours plotting the bulge of a small eyelid, or the extension of a nose from two small holes to a graceful rise of flesh. Then, as if their features had fused inside her when she and Hank lay locked together, she combined in a tiny face his fine nose with her large eyes, his stark cheekbones above her rounded jaw. And when Linda was done she saw she had fully imagined a son.

Hank finally returned, with happy news: while searching for oil deposits he had found in his spare time a fossil fragment of what was possibly a hitherto-unknown branch of ostracoderms, primitive jawless fish. Hank seemed revived by his triumph. He often sat beside her in the evenings, his hands on her belly, attempting to chart unseen growth from a kick, a turn, or a short, insistent pressure, and Linda liked to think that he, too, was conducting an invisible improvisation of their unborn child.

A month later, Linda gave birth and it was a terrible, tearing convulsion—how unnerving that her body could so painfully erupt. And yet now she had a chubby, clutching infant named William. Hank called him Mr. Squeeze and wagged playful fingers above the bassinet, and Linda stared with delight at William's blue eyes, downy hair, and attempted smiles. He was exactly as she had imagined him, her secret thoughts now before her, round and pink and squalling. She could anticipate the smallest flicker of his limbs, she felt his call before he cried. Because of this Linda didn't like to leave her son alone, for if she couldn't see him she sometimes doubted whether he was still there, and she sat by the crib and gorged herself on his quiet breathing.

Hank's skill at uncovering energy deposits and his growing desire to fill gaps in the fossil record continued to take him from home, far away from diaper changes and ear infections, though he insisted he only accepted the most important projects. Lonely while he was gone, Linda tired of the daily rearranging of dust. She felt she was a child again, cooped up in the house because her parents were too worried to let her out where she might catch god knows what. A few of the neighbors on the block kept Linda company while her husband was away, cooing over the baby, offering tips on how to catch up on much-needed sleep, and admiring the large and accumulating display of rocks and fossils. Hank had always returned from each field trip with another new and marvelous rock for Linda: glassy olivine, speckled breccia. But now she saw these gifts as rivals, her rooms decorated with a collection of his geologic infidelities.

Once Hank came home and gave her a simple chunk of gray granite. However, embedded in the middle of one smooth surface was an odd, white smear of quartz that resembled a strange footprint, or perhaps some fleeing thing, or even the ghost of an extinct creature. Linda sat at the kitchen table and stared at her gift, while across from her Hank announced he was Accelerating Soil Creep and nosed their laughing baby across the waxed and slippery floor. But during dinner he was oddly quiet with her.

As they lay in bed together that night, Hank confessed his fear that while he searched for oil, the fossils he really cared for—some perhaps the last of their kind!—were eroding away somewhere beyond recognition or were being crushed underground by tectonic forces. Linda in turn confessed her own unhappiness.

"Why should you be jealous of carbonized graptolites?" Hank

said, stroking her forehead, but Linda suddenly felt buried by
invisible depths of earth. Hank sat up, and when he pulled the
blankets off her slowly, carefully, Linda imagined she was a prize
fossil being uncovered. She allowed him to turn and twist her into
odd shapes. She shook her hair, pretending that the blonde
strands fell into the shape of a brachiopod's patterned ribs or the
many watery arms of a nautiloid, while he entered her again and
again. That night Linda dreamt about the ghostly image in the
center of Hank's latest gift: it grew larger and larger, until she saw
it was one of Hank's teeth, and he was smiling with a mouth so
wide that she found she was falling inside, past his perfect teeth,
falling.

Then Hank was away again, and Linda's days were filled with the
insistent claims of her child, which echoed her own anxious
needs. She often found herself gazing out the window, yet again
at a nearby field that was once ancient forest, at a distant hill that
was no longer mountain. How could the marvelous have become
so routine? Bored with the familiar, malleable earth, Linda stared
at a bare elm across the street. She found herself slowly extending
the branches, and then twisting them into the intricate plumbing
of an invisible house. Hesitant at first, she further imagined
antique, embossed doors and steep gables. This was another form
of geology, she thought: she could hold the invisible past like a
fossil.

Hearing William crying, Linda hurried to his room. Though
she usually liked to stand there by his crib and separate his features, picking out what was Hank's and imagining her husband
was half home, she quickly scooped up William and brought him
back with her. While nursing him she tried to re-create her
apparition, but it had already erased itself. Linda quietly stroked
her son's forehead, frustrated, and she wondered if there were
other unseen territories waiting for her.

Sated, William squirmed in her lap, and Linda looked down at
his restless, excited face. She stuck her tongue out and he laughed.

She did it again, her eyes closed tightly, and she suddenly saw return the shady, encircling porch of the vanished house. William's tiny hands tickled her, and the finely crafted scrollwork on the window shutters etched themselves before her. When his fists pounded aimlessly against her thighs, the house rose up story by story. She held William and bounced him on her knees, happy that this child she had imagined helped her imagine another world.

Everything around her loosened. The doors in her home vibrated, as if still being ripped from a tree. Even when she spoke long-distance to Hank, who was distracted by some worry he wouldn't name, Linda was unable to resist this giddy new world before her and she watched the water glasses in the cabinets evaporate into their original piles of sand.

But soon these pleasures were interrupted when Hank returned home without warning, his car filled with large cardboard boxes. He carried the first one to the door, where Linda met him, and she had to lean across the carton for a kiss. He squeezed past her and walked toward the study. Linda followed and William, just able to walk, wobbled between them.

"Hank, what's the matter?" she asked, but he only grunted.

When he put the box on the floor of the study, he explained that one of his explosions had pulverized a hidden bed of fossils. "The damn company made me keep blasting," he almost shouted. He stood up. "But I did manage to save some."

Linda looked down at the thickly taped box. He had brought the explosion home. She imagined the rocks bursting out of the cardboard packing, each small, sharp piece flying against the walls, and she barely heard Hank say, "I'll just have to salvage what I can." He walked back to the car for another carton, while invisible dust and debris settled over everything.

Because fossils were his first love, Hank explained, he had to take a break from energy freelancing. He worked in his study so relentlessly, surrounded by topographical maps, charts spanning millions of years, and boxes filled with jagged rocks, that he might just as well have been away on another field trip. One afternoon, while William was napping, Linda cautiously entered the study. Hank didn't even look up from his desk.

"Let's play Glacial Melt," she suggested, her hand on the door.

Hank plucked a fossil from a tray. "I don't have any more time for games, Linda," he replied. She left and stood out in the hall, listening to him cleaning fossils with his wire brushes, and she almost wished she was small and hard, so that Hank might hold her too.

At dinner Hank held up the thin, crushed spiral of a gastropod. "Look at this," he said, pointing it at her, "look at what I destroyed." Linda couldn't hold his gaze, so instead she watched the table settings transform themselves—the flower patterns growing off the teapot and plates and twisting around the serving dishes. Why did Hank want to pin down hidden points of time when the true beauty of geology was that past, present, and future bled into each other?

That night Linda waited in bed for Hank. When he didn't appear she decided to fetch him, and she passed through the dark house easily by imagining that the lamps were shining. She opened the door to the study and found Hank exhausted at his desk, among his charts and graphs. There were rocks everywhere, and Linda saw them as huge, pulled teeth. Hank was pressing the eraser end of his pencil against his cheeks, pressing so hard he'd made an odd pattern of red splotches that looked like a strange and terrifying rash.

"Come here," Linda whispered, frightened. Hank looked away without saying a word, but he let her draw him down to the floor, among the clumps of fossils. Her hands stroked his cheeks and forehead and, surrounded by images of extinction, they undressed each other. Her body encircled and accepted him, and at once the succession of small, present moments wasn't enough for Linda to hold on to. She saw the two of them age rapidly into withered shanks and narrow bone, then she saw their limbs grow younger until they were children, wrestling naked on the floor.

Finally she saw them all ages at once—pink cheeks above the wrinkled cords of the neck, firm thighs above bony calves, and their pubic hair dark, then gray. Time circled through them as they shuddered and rocked together, the present moment untethered and wildly swinging back and forth.

Linda woke early in the morning, Hank sleeping in bed beside her, and she remembered the night before. Proud of her abilities, and yet somehow disturbed by this pride, she turned to Hank and quietly confessed to his still back what she had seen during their lovemaking. Sure he would understand, Linda felt infinitely sad that he was still asleep. But then he stirred, his arm reaching out like a gesture from a dream, and his hand gripped hers and tightened.

"What can you possibly be saying?" he asked. Hank reached across the bed for a rock on the night stand. He turned and held it before Linda. "Tell me what you see here," he said.

It was a piece of shale, and embedded in it was a petal-like shape with many feathery arms that seemed to wave, to wave at her, and those motions traveled up Hank's hand, which began to wrinkle, the wrinkles deepening like rivers slowly cutting through shallow hills. She told Hank this, and he looked at the rock as if it had suddenly come alive.

"No," he then said, speaking carefully. "It's a crinoid, an extinct water lily." And he still held it in the air, as if forcing them both to see this.

"Oh, it's more than that, it's geology," Linda replied. She rested her hand over the image in the shale, her fingers touching his.

He frowned. "Geology? C'mon, what are you talking about?"

"What you taught me—that everything changes." And Hank then proved this to be true, for he hurled the rock at the window, bursting it open, and all the pieces of broken glass contained bits of the world outside that changed as they flew through the air.

They cleaned up the room together. Hank kept apologizing,

but Linda laughed at him and picked up a fragment of glass. She twisted it in the light and it framed Hank's anxious face, then their disturbed blankets on the bed, the broken pane, and the scattered glass chips in the rug: Linda's little shard seemed to imagine along with her. "This is wonderful," she told Hank, "and it's all because of you." But he turned away from her and reached carefully for a sliver in the rug.

Linda felt sure she could convince him. But in the following days, whenever she tried speaking to Hank of the secret joys of geology, his face transformed before her into something hard and foreign, like a new rock she had never seen before. "Please, *stop*," he said, interrupting her. Soon his newly salvaged fossils began to appear about the house, on the couch, in the sink, their broken surfaces a solid reproach. About to shower one evening, Linda picked up from the tiled floor of the stall a crooked lump covered with tiny, twisted shells. Linda stared at the patterns until suddenly she was aware of Hank behind her.

"They're dead things, understand?" he said, his voice so oddly unhappy. "They'll *never* come alive."

Linda crouched naked before Hank, afraid, yet she had to tell him how those spiraled shells were undulating in her hand.

Hank began to spend day and night in the study. Linda was anxious for her husband, surrounded inside by so much carefully preserved failure, and she kept watch outside the door. Afraid to imagine what terrible marks he might be making on his face with his pencil, instead she spoke to Hank through the closed door, telling him how the hallway floorboards around her, as if still part of a living tree, sprouted branches and leaves. Wouldn't he like to come out and see them? She could hear him inside brushing away at his fossils with a destructive fury. So she continued, next recounting their son's creation, feature by feature. "Go away!" he screamed from inside. But Linda tried again, describing how his face would change with age, how he would be a beautiful old man. Then there was a long silence, as if he were sitting still in his chair, barely breathing.

* * *

One afternoon while playing with her son in the living room, Linda watched William rock a wicker basket back and forth, back and forth, and she joined in his laughter, for the basket was unraveling and she could see the busy, invisible hands behind it all. Happy for another detail that might attract her husband, Linda walked to the study and was surprised to see the door slightly ajar. She hesitated, then looked inside, but he wasn't at his desk. She entered slowly and saw Hank in the open closet, hanging in the air, the folds of skin on his neck horribly creased around a rope. Linda stared at his feet, inches above the carpeted floor.

Before she could scream, or cry, or even believe what she saw, Linda heard an unhappy shout of her son and his urgent, faltering steps down the hallway. She quickly ran outside and shut the door, standing before it just as William cried into her arms, his small hands on his forehead from some fall. Linda checked and found no bruise. She sank to her knees and hugged him, and his small grief seemed briefly to cancel her own, impending and terrible. She hoped he would never stop crying and held him until he had to break away impatiently. He toddled down the hallway, and she listened to his high laughter in the living room.

Her son gone, Linda leaned against the wall across from the study. She stared at the door and tried to imagine another possibility inside. She tried to reverse everything: the still, hanging body rising from the fall, the neck unsnapping, the hands that had tied the rope's knot now untying it, the quiet steps to the closet now tracing themselves backward to the desk, returning until the first suicidal thought that began it all was not yet thought.

Linda finally entered the study again, and her husband's contorted face stared past her. She rushed out to the living room. William had settled behind one of the upholstered chairs, and she listened to his quiet, self-involved chatter. Then she picked up the phone for an ambulance and started to cry into the humming receiver.

*   *   *

In the weeks following the funeral, Linda found her home had become a new landscape. Each stone of Hank's collection, eloquent in its silence, gave her pain, and she was shaken by the thought that in all her life with him there had been this hidden future, this secret avalanche waiting to fall. But how could she put even one rock away? It would leave another empty space she wouldn't know how to fill. No friends or family could comfort her, and when William woke at night, confused and crying from some bad dream, she ran to him as much to be held as to hold him.

Linda could have gone back to work, but she didn't want to return to cleaning teeth that she knew would eventually decay and collapse in ancient mouths. Instead she stayed home, though everywhere she looked lacked her husband. The handle of Hank's coffee cup had lost his fingers, the rim his lips. Then everything began to crumble. The label of the soup can on the kitchen counter faded and crinkled until its glue dried, the edges curled, and the can itself rusted. The blue wallpaper began to peel like broad, thin shreds of falling sky. The linoleum cracked, and grass grew up past the window sills. Linda sat in a chair and grew old, her fingernails extending until they snapped off, brittle from age. Exposed wooden beams warped and the walls around her sucked in and fell. Then she decayed. The tall grass swayed through her eye sockets and the spaces between her ribs. Metal fillings glinted in her scattered teeth. But then Linda slowly reassembled herself, the ligaments re-forming, the bone adhering to tissue, the veins rethreading themselves throughout her body.

When she was almost whole again she heard a series of crashes in the living room. She hurried to the open doorway and saw William among a pile of rocks, the shelves empty behind him. Linda scolded him and he ran away, laughing a wild laugh, happy to have her attention. She chased him to his room and he stood before her, suddenly about to cry. But then she saw him change into an awkward young man, pimpled and sullen, and suddenly she realized how frighteningly independent he would become. She could see William leaving home, could imagine his infrequent phone calls and large and small lies, imagine, finally, his denial of her in her old age. Crying herself, Linda held out her arms and William, small again, ran to hug her as she knelt down. But patting his back, squeezing his shoulders, she saw a vision of an older boy turning away, ashamed.

Linda grew frightened of her son, his small face a mask insisting itself into her imagination, always about to erupt into the person she feared he would grow to be. When she heard his footsteps now she wanted to run away and at the same time she wanted to run to him, to hide her son's transforming face in her arms. But she was afraid his blonde hair would turn gray beneath the strokes of her hand.

Finally one day Linda found William sneaking up behind her. Strange tremors passed over his face. The curve of his jawline, so much like her own, altered. The furl of nostril that resembled hers erased, and Hank's straight nose pushed forward. She simply vanished from her son's face, while all of Hank's features emerged and twisted themselves older. And then there was her husband, toddling toward her with his arms outstretched, but Linda was already running. She rushed out the front door to the car, ignoring his cries. Shaking in the front seat, she saw Hank in the rearview mirror hurrying down the driveway after her. She started the car, but he slapped at the door again and again, and she had to open it. Her husband stood unhappy before her. She let him in, even though she was fleeing from him.

Hank sniffled and tried to smile, wiping his teary eyes. When Linda leaned across and held his hand he seemed so content that she couldn't imagine now what had ever gone wrong between them. She decided they would take a field trip in the country together and make a new start. Linda drove off, and the immediate sense of escape and the unfolding road were enough to calm her. She turned onto the highway, and with the white lines stretching ahead she felt sure they were both leaving everything terrible behind.

As Linda drove, she pointed, and Hank followed her finger. "Those fields were once a drainage channel, right?" she asked. But Hank played with the straps of his overalls, oddly disinterested. Linda tried again. "How long will it take to erode those hills over there?" Hank only squirmed on the seat beside her, kicking his feet together. Linda gazed off unhappily to the left and saw a runoff ravine in the distance. Though far away, she could make out the crooked trenches of erosion. This would surely interest Hank. She turned off at the first side road, so excited that she swerved sharply at the curve of the exit ramp. Hank abruptly slid across the seat and cried out.

"Sorry, dear," Linda said, slowing down. The new road she took was winding and so full of interesting geologic features that Linda soon lost her way. "Look, a sinkhole!" she called out to her indifferent Hank, who was standing up and about to crawl away from her to the backseat. "A bedding plane, a block fault!" she continued almost desperately.

Searching for topographical features to attract her husband, Linda was having difficulty paying attention to the road. An approaching car honked at her, but Linda saw it was actually an erratic, a huge boulder deposited by a retreating glacier. It passed them before she could point it out to Hank, who had plopped back down on the seat. Linda pressed on the accelerator, entranced by the transforming view of her windshield. Then a truck appeared, but Linda immediately realized it couldn't be that at all. Instead, it was a road cut, and its sheer, towering slabs still frightened her, as they once had so long ago. "There, over there!" she shouted, pointing at the advancing cliff. Her hands tightened on the wheel, ready to turn away, and she fought a growing fascination with the exposed rock, the rippling patterns that seemed about to speak.

Lucky

I have a nice shop—men's clothes, all of them classic. No young kids bother to come in for whatever's latest because they know they won't find it here. I don't mind, I've known most of my regular customers for years—the second anyone walks through the door I can remember his collar size, sleeve length, you name it. I've always been the fellow who tucks everyone nicely into suits and pants and shirts, and I know more than measurements, I know what my customer doesn't want to see in the three-way mirror: usually it's the bald spot, the paunch or the neck wattle, so I divert attention to the shoulder pads, the cuffs, the snappy angle of a lapel.

Maybe I know my customers too well, because when old age settled in and they started dying I took it hard, right from the moment I heard the first bad news. I remember I was standing behind the register, enjoying the look of the long row of suits against the wall—I liked to think they were waiting patiently in line for something, maybe opening night at some big Broadway play, and they were all happy to have tickets. Joe Baxter walked in—the fellow who always goes through the tie racks three times before making up his mind. I was already thinking, Hat size: 7 ¾, when he said, "Hey Pete, guess what?"

He was holding back a nervous grin and I knew I was about to hear some awful surprise—that's just the way he was. He'd done this to me before, once when Sadat was shot, another time when the space shuttle blew up. But Joe stopped smiling when he finally said, "Tiny Martin died—his heart. He just fell down on his way to breakfast."

I leaned back against the counter and could only manage a weak, "No—Tiny? That's terrible." I liked Tiny and always felt sorry for him, beginning with his nickname—he was almost too big for the largest size in the shop. And the poor guy was afraid of the dressing room—he never tried on anything before buying. "No thanks," he said to me the first time he ever stopped by, "I don't need to go in there." So I rearranged the cufflink display while he stood in front of the mirror and held shirts under his chin; after he picked out something, he told some little joke at the register, almost like he was thanking me for leaving him alone. Later, I heard talk that he'd seen real trouble back in the Korean War, squeezed inside some narrow prison cell.

Harriet and I went to his wake—a room full of flowers with nothing cheery about them—and poor Tiny looked awfully cramped in that coffin. The morticians had done a terrible job dressing him—the collar could barely contain his neck, and the knot of his tie was pulled off to one side, just like my brother Jamie's tie at his own funeral so long ago. I hadn't thought of it in years—I was nine, maybe ten, at the time—though I could clearly recall waiting in line for the viewing, nervous even though I knew there was barely a scratch on him—only internal injuries from his fall while chasing me up a tree. Jamie was dressed in a suit—something I'm sure he never wore when he was alive—with a thick blue tie knotted funny and twisted almost sideways. He looked so unlike himself that I leaned up close to his peaceful face, even though I was still afraid: sometimes at night he used to turn on the light by my bed and I'd wake to see his face inches from me, twisted up in some vile and gruesome way until I started crying.

Then there I was, standing beside Tiny's coffin, tears pouring down, and Harriet whispered behind me, "C'mon, honey, people are waiting."

I was so spooked that we left, too early to be polite. After that I avoided wakes and saved my respects for the funeral service, where Harriet and I sat in a pew in the back with the ushers and the less popular relatives. Because there *were* more funerals to go to—Jack Banes, a lover of cardigans, wasted away from cancer; and Paul Markowitz, a tie clip collector, died of kidney failure. Worse, more funerals were on the way. One afternoon I got a call from Gloria, Larry Johnson's wife, and she said, "Pete, Larry needs a shirt for my niece's wedding tomorrow, but he can't, um, come by today. Could you pick something out for him and drop it by later?"

"Sure, I know his size, and you're on my way home," I said, a little surprised, but her tone of voice said, Don't ask questions.

I brought along a nice selection, but Larry was in no condition to choose. He was sitting in the den beside a record player and listening to this scratchy Benny Goodman tune—when the clarinet hit its stride and went in loops around the beat, Larry's face opened up like he was hearing it for the first time. Then he flipped the needle to the beginning so he could hear it for the first time again, and he gave that spinning record a silly grin. This was not at all the same man who rattled off baseball statistics while I chalked cuff lines on his pants. Gloria had a terrible look on her face, like she was a convict counting the minutes before parole, and I knew Larry'd been doing this all day, at least. God knows what was on *my* face, but she leaned in close to me and whispered fiercely. "You think *he's* bad? Tom Peterson is some big fan of *Sesame Street*—he watches letters and numbers dance and sing all day long. Poor Ann."

* * *

So one day I finished my lunch break sandwich, glanced over at the rows of suits, and they looked like they were all lined up to view the deceased. Next thing you know, I might start seeing ghosts poking through shelves of sweaters or avoiding the dressing room. What's needed here is a change of scene, a walk to the park, I told myself, and I tucked the local paper under my arm and closed up shop for the rest of the hour.

I sat on a bench and watched the children playing their games in the sandbox for a while, then I opened up the paper and worked my way into the international news, all that faraway trouble. The national news followed—the usual sleazy dealings in Washington—and then I came to our town's police blotter, the minor local fires, the major sales in the mall. Finally I turned a page and there were the obituaries.

I closed the paper and let it flap in the wind a little bit—after all, I'd come to the park to avoid this sort of thing. But what if someone I knew was in there—was I going to let Joe Baxter surprise me again with another awful grin?

All the names were unfamiliar. How could this upset me? So I read on. Everyone was survived by *somebody:* a wife or husband, brothers or sisters, kids grown up and scattered in different towns or states and *their* kids grown up and scattered. A job was listed too, just like another next-of-kin, and so was the time of death, down to the minute: 12:05 P.M. or 8:34 A.M. or whatever. I thought back to the day before and I tried to remember what I'd been doing at those times: maybe squeezing a tube of toothpaste, or finishing off a tuna sandwich.

That afternoon, when no one was in the shop, I stopped in the middle of arranging a shipment of socks in bins, checked my watch, whispered, "Good-bye and good luck," and wondered if I'd just given a friendly send-off to someone I knew. The next day I read the obits to see how I'd done: no one there was even an acquaintance, and I hadn't even come close to any time of death. But I kept up this little game for weeks, and I began to seem strange to myself.

I started thinking that when I retired—just a few years off, really—Harriet and I should move far, far away, where we didn't know anybody, where the obits wouldn't have one familiar name: I didn't want to wait for Tom Peterson or Larry Johnson or anyone else to die.

Usually when Harriet made breakfast, I watched sleepily and thought about how lucky I was—she could have done a lot better than me, that's for sure. But one morning I finally had to say, "Why don't we move when I retire?"

She kept stirring those scrambled eggs and wouldn't turn around, so I knew I had to speak carefully. Harriet was always the quiet one, and over the years I had learned to read her whole collection of quiets. I even had a favorite, her Out-of-the-Body quiet: I liked watching her knit, hands on automatic while her face took on this kind of faraway peace, like she could see something really wonderful that was miles off.

But the way she was slowly stirring those eggs I knew she was into her I-Wish-You-Hadn't-Said-That quiet.

"Say we move south," I said to the back of her head. Her hair was up in its usual bun, with a wisp loose here and there—I still loved it when she let it down. "Think of all that sun. And there'd be no snow. If we moved we could have a yard sale and sell the snow shovel and ice scraper, we could donate our boots and gloves and coats to the Salvation Army." I hoped this might soften her up—Harriet could never get warm enough in the winter.

"What about the children?" she asked.

"I don't know, what about them? They can learn to send their postcards to a new address, dial a different area code, I guess." Harriet was suddenly real busy dishing out the eggs and about to settle into her If-You're-not-Going-to-Be-Serious-I'm-not-Going-to-Listen quiet, and she was right. We'd raised two fine kids—a girl and boy—and our worrying over each scraped knee, every chickenpox scar, and all the other marks the world made on them was not something to joke about. So I added, "Look, honey, if we lived in Florida we'd be closer to Elizabeth and the boys. And Jimmy can afford to travel a little farther."

"What about my bingo?" she said.

Harriet was quite the popular bingo caller, in demand at the Legion and the Moose Lodge, Am Vets, Elks, and even the Catholic church, but I can't say I much approved of her hobby. In those days even a lottery ticket was too much of the gambling world for me. So I said, though gently, "What, you think this is the only town where people play bingo? You can do that anywhere."

By then Harriet was looking out the window, filled with her I'll-Consider-It quiet, so I let the subject drop and considered myself lucky: I knew if I had to tell Harriet my secret reason for leaving she'd laugh, might even talk me out of it. But I didn't want to be laughed at, and I didn't want to be talked out of anything.

Maybe the thought of moving made Harriet want to settle in more and take hold of the house as she never had before, because the next Saturday morning she started listening to this crazy radio program about how to express yourself everywhere in the home, the host's slick voice just slipping along: "Why settle for the ugliness of commercial packaging in your home? Pour the milk you buy out of its carton and into your own brightly colored plastic containers. Think how much nicer Cheerios look in mason jars. Ladies, get rid of all that advertising, take control. After all, it's your home and no one else's."

Harriet took notes at the kitchen table. I left the room, depressed that I was driving my wife to such silly behavior. But no matter where I wandered in the house I could still hear the murmur of that cheery voice, so I went out for a long stroll. I walked through the falling leaves, kicking past little piles here and there, and I headed for the used bookstore to see if I could find some light reading.

Usually there'd be a tempting book in the window display, but that morning, when I glanced at the plain black cover of *Strategic Solitaire,* I decided I wasn't really interested in learning how to outwit a pack of cards. Next to this was a book of photographs about steam engines—I wouldn't have minded a train taking me far away, but not one that didn't exist any more. Then I looked at a book on hunting decoys, a beautiful wooden duck on the cover, and I thought about all the time and cunning it took to carve such a thing.

Finally, I turned to an anatomy book. Its cover was a drawing of a man's head arched back a bit, eyes closed and face so peaceful, but he was dead, a cadaver. The skin of his neck was sliced open and pulled back to show a tangle of veins, muscles, and nerves, packed together like wires in a telephone cable. I couldn't take my eyes off that cover. Behind me I heard the purr and rattle of a few cars passing by, a bicycle with baseball cards clicking the spokes, and a couple of running, rowdy kids, as if the world were saying, Keep walking, *move on.*

But I did go inside, though at first I picked up a book on the solar system and found myself staring at those fantastic *Voyager* pictures from Neptune: that dark storm spot and its clouds, the ice volcanoes on one of the big moons, the thin, wobbly rings. All the while I scratched an itch on my neck and imagined the veins inside.

I decided I might as well give the damned anatomy book a peek if I was going to keep thinking about it. Soon I was seriously staring at those drawings: the heart a collection of bloody caves, red and blue veins winding their way everywhere, nerves branching crazily all through the face, and pale intestines bunched up like thick clouds. There were even glands under the eyelids that looked like ferns, and I blinked, teary eyed, amazed that this was all just beneath my skin—even the edge of the solar system didn't seem as strange.

I bought the book and brought it home. Harriet was out for the week's shopping and I sat on the couch, turning the pages to lymph glands clinging to abdominal muscles. I discovered my body was a bucket of words I could barely pronounce. The tongue alone was covered with words like Hylo-glossus, fibrous septum, and the sulcus terminalis, and then I came upon this: "After completing the dissection of the preceding muscles, saw through the lower jaw just external to the symphysis. Then draw the tongue forward, and attach it, by a stitch, to the nose; then its muscles, which have thus been put on the stretch, may be examined."

I slammed the book shut and stared at nothing until I heard Harriet park in the driveway. Before hurrying out to help her with the groceries, I hid the book under the couch. I didn't want her to see what I'd seen.

Though I didn't mention moving again to Harriet, I left the travel section of the newspaper lying open to articles like "Florida Wonderland" and "The Pleasures of Savannah." Time had to be on my side—we were well into fall and it was getting colder every day. But Harriet just sat by the radio with her I'm-All-Ears quiet. "Buy three or four different frozen pizzas and slice them up *before* you store them," that smoothie purred on, "this way you can mix and match to put together your very own combinations." Pretty soon, whenever I opened the refrigerator or checked the cabinets I saw single scoops of ice cream sealed in baggies, bars of unwrapped butter stacked like a pyramid on a plate, split pea soup exposed in a glass jar.

On Halloween night Harriet prepared her own special sandwich bags of candy corn. But whenever the doorbell rang I felt I was carrying little piles of pulled and rotten teeth to the monsters at my front stoop. The little hands of vampires, witches, and mummies reached up to me with their bags and I held them off, even the scary skull face.

I stood in the doorway and watched them retreat into the dark street, recounting to myself the sutures of the skull—the sagittal and squamo-parietal. Then I returned to my chair in the living room and imagined my own Halloween costumes inside me: the ligaments of my hands mummy bandages, the banded muscles on my face like that Freddy Krueger. I was my own House of Horrors, with too many secret passageways. Soon I dreaded the thought of the doorbell ringing again.

Even at work I'd get cranked up like this, and no busy fooling with the cufflink rack or flipping through my order slips could keep me from imagining the curve of the spine down the back of a mannequin. One day, just after I'd noted the time and whispered "au revoir" to whoever, Danny Williams came in and I was happy to see him, I waited for him to start his routine. Danny liked to finger his way through practically everything in the store until suddenly he'd march over to the one place he hadn't poked through—say, the tie clasps—and pick out something in two minutes.

But that afternoon he was collecting shirts, three or four nicely tailored ones, and for once the usual worry was wiped from his face. At the register he said, "I hit the lottery big this week, Pete—a thousand bucks, my best yet."

"Congratulations," I said, but Danny wasn't listening, and though he was staring right at me, he wasn't seeing *me*—he was already in another shop, picking whatever he liked off the shelves.

That was just the sort of distraction I needed—whiling away the hours toting up the prize money I might win. And why not me? "Miracles can happen," my mother used to tell me, at least until Jamie died, until she was hunched over on the couch and sobbing over the brother who never did anything but beat me up or frighten me whenever he had the chance. When my father shouted, "*Playing?* You're lucky to be alive!" his voice might as well have been miles away—I was still scrambling up that tree, away from all the terrible things Jamie said he was going to do when he caught me, and just when I was sure he'd grab my ankle there were no more threats, only the sound of branches snapping, and when I looked below me he was lying on his back on the ground.

So I was lucky. Still, when I bought that first lottery ticket I didn't tell Harriet—she knew I thought her bingo nights were a little silly. But this was different—every time I thought of the veins crisscrossing my hand like a bloody glove, I'd finger the ticket in my pocket and it was more than a slip of paper, it was really five, ten, fifteen million dollars, whatever. All I had to do was close my eyes and it became a trip around the world, or a yacht, and I could even afford not to learn how to sail—I'd hire someone to navigate me wherever I'd like! I'd set up a fat wad for the kids and grandkids, buy a big new house far away from here and retire early.

I waited for each weekly announcement on the local news, but when the numbers flashed I lost my imagined fortune and I was holding just a little piece of colored paper in my hands. Then I moped around, waiting for Harriet to leave on an errand so I could leaf through the anatomy book like some kid with his porno magazine. But I suppose I just gave off misery—Harriet didn't like to leave me alone and I had to settle for hiding behind the paper and reading the obits. How could I explain my trouble? Whenever I thought of confessing to Harriet, I imagined my tongue pulled out and stitched to my nose.

One Friday evening I trudged up the steps home, barely able to face another weekend with that book I couldn't throw away, and Harriet was waiting for me at the door, deep into her It's-Time-to-Put-a-Stop-to-Whatever-This-Is quiet. "Let's go to the diner tonight," she said.

This surprised me—Friday was usually one of her bingo nights, but I didn't hesitate long enough to start Harriet's Don't-Argue quiet. Sometimes we like to eat at the diner and listen to the people in the booths next to us—there's something about a booth that makes people believe they're all alone and nobody's eaves-dropping. So I said, "Sure thing."

We stood at the entrance and smelled the country ham, listened to the crack and bubble of fries cooking in oil, and we scanned the booths. Slim pickings: a family of squawling kids, a couple of

loners reading newspapers and shoveling food. Then Harriet
gave me a little sideways glance, nodded her head at a young couple leaning into each other, and we were ready for whispered love
talk.

We sat down and spread open the menus, thumbing the smooth
laminated pages. I ordered Salisbury steak with that sweet, thick
gravy, Harriet ordered the fried chicken, on special. Next door
the couple was cooing, and even an overheard "Pass the salt"
gave me gooseflesh. Harriet looked out over the long counter, the
long sizzling grill behind it, and she wore just the tiniest smile, her
We-Shouldn't-Be-Doing-This quiet slowly turning into her
Isn't-This-Wonderful quiet. She reached out for my hand, I
squeezed back, and we were young again. When dinner came it
tasted better than it should have: Harriet sliced through the crispy
skin of her chicken, I scooped up forkfuls of mashed potatoes.

But suddenly those kids were arguing, their voices all screwed
up with angry love. "I can't stand it any more," he said, though I
could tell from his voice that he had miles and miles to go before
he reached his limit.

"Why do you always say that?" she said, but she knew the
answer, she was just giving him a chance to repeat it.

They kept bickering, but even this was romantic. Harriet and I
eyed each other as we ate, remembering the kinds of arguments
we used to have long ago, arguments about nothing—the kind we
couldn't even remember though we'd wake up in the morning
with our throats hoarse from all that shouting, and then we'd just
have to press against each other until the alarm rang.

They were finally quiet next door, except for the young fellow's fingers tapping away anxiously on the table. The tick of his
fingernail made a sad little echo inside me, and I saw the bone
encased in muscle, the little pumping capillaries swirling around
just beneath the skin, all of it wrapped so tightly together.

The waitress was standing by my shoulder with a full pot of
coffee. "No thanks," I said, "and no dessert, either—just the
check, please." Harriet stared at me, surprised, but I could only
say, "I don't feel so good. Must have been those string beans." I

turned away, suddenly interested in the polished curves of the revolving stools by the counter and how they distorted everything in the diner, even Harriet with her I-Thought-You-Loved-Me quiet. I did, I did, but my tongue felt so thick in my mouth.

When I lay in bed next to Harriet that night she reached out and stroked the space between my shoulder blades—that old, familiar gesture—and she whispered, "Let's go Siamese." But how could I? I didn't want to think of us together as two sacks of blood and bones, our stomachs digesting against each other, the muscles contracting beneath our lips. I just had to pretend I was asleep.

So I lay there on my back, eyes closed but utterly awake as though I were a kid again, waiting in the dark for Jamie's footsteps, hoping to catch him before he frightened me with one of his twisted faces: if all I heard was steady breathing, I'd sneak to his bedside and stare at his sleeping face. All the meanness was gone, he looked like a different brother, more like the one I wanted. I wished he'd never wake up, and when I looked down at him during his wake and knew he never would, I was afraid my nighttime wishes had caused his death.

I did *not* want to think about this and I rustled in bed beside Harriet's soft breathing, but there was Jamie, tucked into a suit in a coffin where he couldn't get at me, his face so peaceful, his powdered skin stretching and thinning until his skull shone through and grinned at me.

I bolted up in bed—after all these years Jamie had scared me again. I wanted to wake up Harriet and hold her, but what would I tell her? So instead I made faces at the dark, grimaced until my jaws ached, my eyes watered.

I slept late, and when I walked down the stairs to the kitchen I heard the theme music of that smooth talker on the radio. He was reeling off the usual: "Remember, nothing is too small to bear your imprint, your own special flair for organization in the home." Harriet stood at the counter, plucking grapes from their crooked stems—the whole bunch looked like a lung she was tearing apart.

It was no hard choice to skip breakfast. I drove off to the stationery store for my lottery ticket, and as I slipped in and out of traffic I was really roaring through the bloodstream, past blood cells and antibodies, and the telephone wires and bare tree branches above were a network of nerves and ganglia. Then I knew there was no escape: the entire world was a body turned inside out, and wherever I moved it would look the same.

When I returned home Harriet had more nonsense spread out before her: carefully cut little squares of cellophane and a pile of individually wrapped grapes. I listened to the little crinkles of clear plastic and I was about to say, I'll stay put, just *please* stop listening to that damned radio. But Harriet turned to me, her embarrassed face crumpled up and filled with a quiet I had never seen before, and she said, "This must be the silliest thing I've ever done."

"I think I agree with you there, honey," I replied. We stood across from each other, both so unhappy. I put my hand in my pocket and crumpled up the lottery ticket, and all day my fingers kept at the thing until it was a moist little pellet, no bigger than a spitball. I stared at a few football games, but I didn't even know what teams were playing, and I didn't care who won, who lost.

When Harriet slipped clothes in the dryer downstairs or ironed in the sewing room, I managed to keep myself from sneaking peeks at the circulatory system. But soon she'd be off for bingo, and I knew I'd be turning page after page if I were left alone. I'd never gone with Harriet before—my excuse was always my long day at the shop—but now I lingered at the door to the bedroom while she put up her hair, and I asked, "Mind if I come along tonight?"

A good crowd filled the long tables in the Am Vets basement. Cigarette smoke was everywhere—old ladies, young marrieds, and assorted fatsos were puffing that big room into cloudy skies and I thought, So *this* is what my wife doesn't want to give up?

The cashier grinned through his wrinkled face and shook my hand when Harriet introduced me, and he said, "Ah, the Mystery Husband, we're so pleased to finally meet you. You're in for a treat tonight."

"Y'think so? Maybe I'll hit the jackpot?"

"Anything's possible," he said, handing me six bingo cards for my five dollars. Harriet walked up front and settled down beside a big glass box half-filled with white balls. Soon she was surrounded by a group making quiet happy talk and—suddenly shy—I left her alone.

I parked at one of those long tables like a kid in a school cafeteria, about to suffer overcooked peas. I read the list of the evening's jackpots—mostly fifty to one-hundred dollars—and peeked over at the lady next to me in a large faded dress. She whispered to herself, pushing the little colored plastic panels over the numbers on her bingo cards while she fingered her stringy hair. All around her were little dolls and more than a few crucifixes—this woman was trying to attract some serious good luck. I glanced down at my own cards. They had advertising on them— for a notions shop, a funeral home. No, this just won't do, I thought, about to sneak out for a two-hour walk somewhere, until I felt the hush in the room.

Harriet held a microphone, and in that glass case the air-cushioned balls were bouncing away. "All right, everyone, time to begin," she said, and she grabbed one of the white balls, read it, and called out the number: "G–56 . . ., G–five-six . . ."

Her voice sounded strange through the PA system—closer and farther away at the same time. I checked my cards for the number, waited for the next one, and then checked again, pushing those little plastic panels here and there. At the next table a black kid with one of those flat-top hairdos grumped, "She's off her stride tonight." I thought, How could anyone screw up numbers? She sounded all right to me.

I kept up fine with my six cards, and across from me a lady scanned over twenty. Everywhere heads were bent, and I suspected that some rent payments might be riding on tonight's jackpots. Pretty soon a woman near the front shouted out "Bingo!" A checker strolled by—looked like he might double as a bouncer—and called out the woman's numbers.

"That's a good one," Harriet announced.

Then we were on to a second round of straight bingo, and after that a variation, where the numbers had to form a diamond shape. The next game was the Letter X Special for a double jackpot, and when Harriet started calling out numbers again—"B–10 . . ., B–one-zero . . ."—the place started to buzz a little. "She's finally warming up," the stringy-haired woman beside me murmured.

I listened more closely to Harriet's voice and caught a little flutter I'd never heard before. She probably knew everyone here and how badly they needed to win, and I guessed she was happy that everyone listened to her, that they couldn't wait to hear what number she'd announce next.

She didn't disappoint, she kept calling out numbers with just the right pause: my wife always had a way with quiet, and the sound of her voice—"I–16 . . ., I–one-six"—was a gentle rocking. So this was what I'd missed all these years.

I sat back in my chair and looked up at her. Just by the way her head tilted slightly I could see, even from far away, that her face was filled with a funny kind of waiting, and then she was into her Out-of-the-Body quiet. But she was still calling out numbers—"O–63 . . ., O–six-three"—and I heard something else in her voice, a kind of music more complicated than all of her quiets: those numbers had words in them, whole sentences, long speeches. Harriet was talking to herself, and all of us in that big room were only eavesdropping while she said, *This could be the one, your big chance, here it comes and it's better than money, it's good luck, maybe even a new life, and I'll say the number you're waiting for, see?—I won't keep it, I'll give it to you, it's yours, not mine.*

Like everyone else in the room, I wanted that luck. But it

wasn't in a winning number—let somebody else shout *Bingo*—it was in Harriet's voice. I wanted her to keep calling out those numbers forever so I could listen as she floated out of herself. And I wasn't crazy, everybody around me seemed to catch the same thing I did—I swear some people were even swaying slightly. Swaying a little myself, I actually tapped my fingers on the table in time to the rhythms of her voice, and I just knew I could tap them all evening and listen to Harriet, I could come back week after week for more: I could be a regular.